Nathan Birr

Presents

SHADES

Published by Beacon Books

Stock media for cover provided by m2art/Shutterstock.com

ISBN: 978-1-7374270-9-4 (sc)

www.nathanbirr.com

ALSO BY NATHAN BIRR

The Douglas Files
Overnight Delivery
Three's a Crowd
All an Illusion
Shot List
Chasing the Wind
Blood and Treasure
One Life to Lose
Golden Key
Mine to Avenge
Nine Lives

Douglas Files Shorts
Black Male
WinterKill
Short Sail
As Good As Dead

The Last Resort Series
Fire & Ice
Broken Trust
The Fountain
Backs Against the Wall

Standalone Stories
God, Girls, Golf & the Gridiron
(Not Always in That Order) . . .
A Love Story

The Book of Levi

All is Calm?

Augusta Whispers

Final Rest

Non-Fiction
Rights or Wrong? Examining the
Declaration of Independence in
the Light of Scripture

www.nathanbirr.com

To Dad, who introduced me to The A-Team, MacGyver, Magnum, P.I., *and* The Rockford Files, *and who let me stay up late on school nights to watch reruns of the same. The credit—or the blame, depending on how you look at it—for this book ultimately goes to him. Love you, Pops!*

ONE

I DON'T BELIEVE IN FATE—NOT AS SOME OVERRULING, ALL-

powerful entity, at least. And while I've heard that the Lord works in mysterious ways, this didn't seem like His style. Nor, can I say, after careful reflection, that I homed in on something triggered by my highly active subconscious. To be sure, I've done that before, but this wasn't that. As much as I hate to admit it, the reason for me making initial contact can only possibly point back to one thing:

The girl was cute.

She wasn't alone. There were, and always are, a lot of beautiful young women—and some not so young—lounging around the pools at The Grandeur Hotel and Resort. Don't get me wrong, I'm not some sort of creep who leers at women in swimwear from behind palm trees (although I did bust a guy for that once). But the scenery is a significant perk of working at one of Miami's premier resort properties as opposed to, say, being surrounded by women in parkas ice skating outside the Royal Scandinavian Hotel in St. Paul.

I also don't make a habit of trying to pick up female guests. I'm not above a little flirting or even the occasional lunch or dinner date. I am a red-blooded, twenty-five-year-old male, after all. But, as the hotel detective—officially the Head Security Officer—at the resort, I try to maintain professionalism. That said, I do strike up conversations with a lot of guests, of both sexes, in an effort to get to know the hotel's clientele. You'd be surprised how many would-be miscreants and troublemakers can be identified by observing their behavior from afar or from a few minutes of chitchat.

But I can't say it was a desire to get a feel for the weekend's guests that caused me to approach the girl either. That *was* my reason for wandering by her a little before ten a.m. on a summer Friday morning. Fridays are my favorite time at the resort. The Grandeur offers special extended-weekend rates, drawing in a lot of guests from along the Eastern seaboard who fly in late Thursday and stay through Sunday. On Friday morning, they slowly come to life and crawl out of their suites to swim, sunbathe, hit the beach just a few dozen yards east, or take advantage of the property's amenities. You can almost feel the anticipation hanging in the air like the morning mist. That's why I break from tradition (and my better judgment) on Friday mornings and get up early. I have some breakfast on the patio of the villa on the north edge of the property where I live, leisurely drink some coffee while reading the *Herald*, and then make my rounds.

The resort flows across nearly seven acres of barrier island between the Atlantic Ocean and Biscayne Bay. The hotel itself is seven stories tall, shaped in a gentle arc running away from the ocean and culminating in a circular, two-story atrium that hosts the front desk, gift shop, a bar, a cutting-edge smoothie and juice bar, and access to the hotel's meeting rooms. A separate building houses the resort's two restaurants, with food also served at the hotel rooftop bar during select hours. An ice cream shop/old-fashioned soda parlor sells an assortment of candies and treats, and room service is available round the clock.

As far as amenities go, the resort features tennis, basketball, and sand volleyball courts; shuffleboard; an indoor game room and lounge; a barbershop and hair salon; a small spa; and a clubhouse. Two swimming pools, three hot tubs, a firepit, and a tranquil English-style garden are all nestled among hundreds of palm trees that provide a canopy—while still letting in plenty of Florida sunshine—that creates a sense of seclusion in the midst of the hustle and bustle of Miami Beach. There's good reason why the rich (and sometimes the famous) make The Grandeur their South Florida getaway, and also why the resort employs a full-time detective.

But try telling that to Summer Dawson. She's the resort manager, and usually my first stop on Friday mornings. She lets me know if there are any VIPs or other guests who might require attention and gives me a rundown of any goings on at the resort for the weekend. She also gives me a hard time about everything from politics to my apparel to the necessity of my existence on the grounds. (To be fair, I give her plenty of guff in return). Sometimes, I skip our check-in altogether, knowing she'll find me if there's something important. For no other reason than I'd spent more time reading the *Herald* (a deep dive on the political aspects of the Soviet-led boycott of the upcoming L.A. Olympics) than normal, on this Friday I blew her off and headed for the pools.

I was overdressed in a lemon-yellow Winchester shirt, white chinos, and horsebit loafers, but my mother taught me to never apologize for looking sharp. I was also in danger of getting hot, which is why I strolled leisurely and kept in the shade as much as possible. Until I saw the girl.

She was seated on a cushioned wood chaise lounge on the southeast corner of the west pool. She wore a pink one-piece swimsuit, practically prudish compared to others around her. A full-length floral cover-up hung off her shoulders and draped over the sides of the chair as she sat, one knee bent, reading a magazine. A straw hat with a white ribbon around it wasn't anything fancy, but there was something about the way it rested atop wavy chocolate-brown hair that made me take a second look. Like I said, she was cute, but so were any of a dozen other women in the vicinity. Yet as I circled the pool, I couldn't stop glancing her way. Maybe it was the hat.

She was alone, judging by the empty chairs on either side and the fact that the table to her right held only one glass of orange juice and only one folded towel. I checked the time on my gold Rolex—ten on the button—and shuffled over. I stopped in front of the chair on her left. "Mind if I sit down?" I asked.

The girl—and she couldn't have been much over twenty—lifted her chin and turned toward me. I tried not to wince when I saw her sunglasses—a cheap plastic pair that screamed of having been bought in the grocery store checkout line as an afterthought. Her chin rose a fraction more, probably because she had taken notice of my hair. I am vain about few things in life, but my slightly wavy, light-brown flow is one of them.

"Not at all," she said in a soft voice, her tone neither inviting nor dismissive.

I sat sideways on the edge of the next chaise lounge. "I like your hat," I said.

Her mouth wanted to break into a smile, but all she managed was a "Thanks." She turned her head back down toward her magazine, *People*, with Sly Stallone and Dolly Parton embracing on the cover. I was about to consider it a brushoff—it happens to the best of us—when she said, after licking her finger and turning a page and without looking up, "I like your hair."

I grinned. I told you, Don Johnson wishes he had such a mane.

She closed the magazine and turned toward me again. "I'm Gia."

"Shades," I answered. It drew the expected frown and a raised eyebrow as she pulled down her sunglasses. They had been concealing dark brown almond eyes, another reason the sunglasses should have been relegated to the trash heap.

Gia looked at me for a second, likely seeing her reflection in the orange and purple gradient of my Porsche Design by Carrera aviator sunglasses. "Shades?" she finally said.

I nodded.

"I'm guessing that isn't what your mother calls you."

"No," I said, folding my hands as my forearms rested on my knees. "She and my father stuck me with the name Gregg."

"That isn't so bad."

"They used three Gs. Greg-g."

"Mmm," she said, tipping her head to the side and back, "that does seem a little excessive." Then she looked back at my sunglasses. "Do you wear those to match the moniker, or are they the reason for it?"

"My buddy Kevin gave me the nickname. I've got sensitivity to sunlight, so I wear them all the time. And I'm sort of a snob about sunglasses."

"So you wouldn't, for example, wear these?" she asked, holding up her cheapies.

"I wouldn't be caught dead in them," I said, then smiled.

"Ow," she said. Then she shrugged. "Neither would I, but I couldn't find mine when we left. My brother bought me these in the airport."

"When did you arrive?"

"Nine . . . thirty? last night," she said. "You?"

"Fall of 1980."

She frowned again, and it wasn't unattractive.

"I work here," I said. "I'm the hotel detective."

Gia laughed.

I indulged it with a lopsided smile.

She stopped laughing and narrowed her gaze. "You're serious?"

"I am."

"What does a hotel detective do, besides what they show on the old black-and-white movies?"

I gave her the standard answer, about helping guests feel secure, keeping an eye out for petty thieves and making sure everyone behaved and . . . the occasional busting of a creep.

"Is that why you came over, because I looked like I might misbehave?"

"No, I told you, I like your hat."

"That was a gift from my brother too. He said it fit me."

"That it does."

Gia smiled wide, revealing perfect white teeth.

"Your brother, he's here with you?"

"He's golfing. Allegedly a business venture."

"That what brought you to South Florida?"

"No, he just finds business everywhere he goes. Kind of odd, really." She briefly extended her arms, causing the baggy sleeves of her cover-up to fall back above her elbows. "My grandfather actually sprang for the trip. He's meeting some old associates and brought us along."

"Nice."

"Yes and no. He's hanging out with them all day. I think they were off to play shuffleboard—is there anything that screams old geezer more than playing shuffleboard?—and Tony heads to the golf course right away, so here I sit by myself. And a girl can only laze by the pool so long."

"You don't swim?"

"I'll take a dip, but how long can that last? Besides," she said, giving me a leering grin, "I'm afraid someone will come along while I'm in the pool and steal my hat."

"Leave your sunglasses on top of it to scare thieves off."

Gia stuck out her tongue.

I beamed.

"Isn't it *your* job to keep it safe?"

"Touché."

"Where did you buy those sunglasses, anyhow? I need to get a better pair. I think some snot-nosed kid fingered these on the rack before Tony bought them."

I reached for the silver stem of my sunglasses and slid them off my face. "Have mine."

"I can't take yours."

"Sure." I shrugged. "I've got other pairs." I extended them to her. "Go ahead."

"I can't."

"At least try them on," I said. "They'll look great with that hat."

With an embarrassed smile, Gia took my sunglasses, shook them slightly so the stems were spread wide, and threaded them through the curls of hair beside her face. Then she turned to me.

"They're you," I said. "Keep them."

"Are you sure?"

"Positive."

"You'll go blind."

"Hardly. I'll squint my way back to my villa and get another pair."

"Here," she said, handing me hers. "Wear these back."

Because I thought it might make her laugh and because I liked Gia's laugh—and *only* for that reason—I put them on. "These are smudged."

"And hideous," she said.

I took them off and quickly and stuffed them in my shirt pocket, lest anyone see me in them.

"Thank you . . . So I just call you 'Shades'?"

"Most everybody does."

"Thank you, Shades."

"You're welcome, Gia." I slapped my knees. "I'll let you get back to your *Rhinestone* review. I should make my rounds and see if there are any other hats that need protecting."

"Hard work, but somebody has to do it."

I grinned. "Enjoy your quick swim."

"I'll try."

I stood, then stopped. "How long is your brother golfing?"

Gia shrugged. "He's playing eighteen, so early afternoon?"

"If you don't have any other plans, would you like to have lunch with me?"

She looked up at me, as if contemplating. Then she said, "Yeah, I would."

"About twelve-thirty?"

"Okay."

"Meet me by the Circle Bar," I said as I gestured over my shoulder with my thumb.

"Okay," she said again.

"Enjoy your swim," I said, this time sincerely. As I turned and headed for my villa, I had two things in mind: One, justification for doing what I so rarely did, making a date on a whim with a guest. Two, how quickly I could dispose of Gia's cheap sunglasses and outfit myself with a decent pair again.

TWO

As it turned out, I met another woman at the

Circle Bar.

Extended from the deck between the two pools, the bar catches the eye of thirsty swimmers and sunbathers, as well as anyone heading to or from the beach or looking out from north-facing suites. It is very cleverly named for the semicircular bar, with seating for twenty under a canopy made to resemble a giant beach umbrella—without being kitschy. Another dozen or two people can crowd around tables set around the bar. Late afternoons, it is packed.

At quarter after ten, as I looped back from around the east pool, most of the seats at the bar or around it were empty. One very noticeably was not. A woman in a long, navy-blue dress sat near the middle of the circle, facing sideways so she could rest one elbow on the bar. Her left leg was crossed over the right knee, revealing a silver high-heeled sandal. It matched bangles on her left wrist and a watch on her right, drop earrings, and a diamond pendant necklace that dangled just above the cut of her dress. Black, straight hair was drawn back in a tight, low ponytail, and frameless round sunglasses—with silver stems—were propped on top of her drawn back hair. I put her at forty, maybe forty-five, but having lost none of her youthful beauty.

I would like to tell you she was drawn to *my* good looks, regal stature, and sharp threads, but she actually turned her head to follow the outstretched arm of Guy, a French expat who tended the various bars at The Grandeur. He pointed me out as I passed, then waved and signaled for me to come over. As I approached, the woman took a sip from a tall glass of clear liquid, then pivoted on her stool.

"Are you the house detective?" she asked in staccato speech. She sounded like someone who *had* had an accent at one point, but her English was flawless.

I nodded and extended my hand. "Shades."

"Diana Berglowe. Mr. Shades, could we speak privately?"

Guy had gone back to buffing the far end of the counter, and there were only two other guests under the canopy, but it wasn't me looking for solitude. I nodded and offered my hand to help her from the stool. She stood—she was only a few inches shorter than my six-one—and reached into a purse on her right shoulder. It too was silver, small and chic, and she drew several bills and placed them on the bar. Then she turned back to me. "Lead the way, Mr. Shades."

I didn't bother to correct her, and instead—noting no ring on her finger—offered her my elbow. She clasped it and we walked slowly through the palm trees down the path leading to the large live oak that served as something of a hub for the grounds. "What brings you to The Grandeur, Miss Berglowe?" I asked.

"Diana, please."

I bowed my head slightly.

"Just a long weekend getaway," she said.

"Did you arrive last night?"

"Technically this morning."

"Where from?"

She hesitated, and I looked her way. We took a few synchronized steps, and her lips parted in a smile. "Dallas, Texas."

"You don't sound like a Texan," I said.

"I try not to."

I grinned, then nodded at a wooden bench swing set off from the sidewalk on the right. Two coconut palms flanked it and, while they did little to provide actual privacy, they gave a sense of it. So did the lack of others on the path or nearby lawn, which separated us from the pool deck. "Will this suffice?" I asked.

"I think so," she said, and I again extended a hand as she sat down.

I sat on her left. "What can I do for you?"

We rocked very gently for a moment before she answered. "Mr. Shades, I am a wealthy woman, and as such, I am afforded certain whims and vanities."

She said it as if it were an accepted fact, and I didn't disagree.

"One of them is traveling with a genuine cultured-pearl necklace. It was a gift from an . . . a liaison several years ago, and its sentimental value rivals its financial one, which is considerable," she said with an upturn of her near eyebrow. She looked down at her lap, where her hands were clasped tightly. "Perhaps it is nothing more than paranoia, but I can't help feel . . . anxiety at the thought of losing it." She looked back up, directly at me, and I was drawn to her vivid blue eyes, clichéd as that may have been. "I was hoping you might provide me some sense of security as to its safety."

I couldn't help but wonder if Diana's late-night flight from Dallas had shown a noir movie, one of those old black-and-whites Gia had mentioned. Then again, who was I to talk, the way I was being drawn into those eyes?

"Where is the necklace?" I asked.

"In the safe in my suite," she answered.

"If I may, do you intend to wear it while you're here?"

"I can't say. Very likely—that's why I prefer to have it with me. A woman never knows what occasion might arise—and thus what clothing and what accessories may be necessary."

"Is your concern for the necklace when it's in the safe or while it graces your neck?"

"To be candid, Mr. Shades, all the time."

"I could offer you my safe, but it's no more secure than the one in your suite, or the house safe in the hotel office, but I'm afraid neither of those would be very convenient for you."

"No, I suppose not. And I don't mean to imply that you should serve as my bodyguard, but I wonder if it wouldn't be too much for me to ask that you . . . at least keep an eye out?"

"For . . . ?"

"Any suspicious characters, or anyone who seems to be lurking or . . ." She swallowed ". . . following me."

I concealed a grin. The house detective tracking jewel thieves was a stereotype, perhaps, but nothing more. However, Diana Berglowe seemed like a woman who would be assured less by logic and more by platitudes. So I indulged her.

"Of course," I said with a nod. "I will maintain a watchful eye."

She broke into another smile.

"Are you aware of anyone who might pose a threat? I don't mean to sound impudent, but are you traveling alone?"

"I am."

"Are you planning to rendezvous with anyone here?"

"No."

"No expectations that anyone who might pose a threat will be here?"

"No." She looked down again. "I must seem to you a foolish old woman."

"Not at all foolish," I said, "and certainly not old."

Diana lifted her chin, the smile returning.

"I will keep an eye out," I said, "but I'm sure you have nothing to fear."

"Thank you, Mr. Shades."

"My pleasure," I said.

We stood. I asked if I could walk her somewhere, and she said she was going back to her suite to rest before lunch. We shook hands, and I clasped hers briefly, assuring her again that her pearls would be safe. Then we parted, and I again set out for my villa, unable to shake the feeling that there was something more to Diana's request for help. I couldn't put my finger on it—maybe it was nothing more than her paranoia creating paranoia in me that there *was* a jewel thief on the premises. Or maybe it was a grown, mature woman playing the part of the damsel in distress, everything but the fluttering eyelashes.

I didn't have long to think about it. It took less than five minutes to walk to my villa along the back hedge of the property. Enough ferns, hydrangeas, dwarf and sand palms, not to mention trunks and low-hanging palm fronds, made it so that each villa's front door and patios were more or less secluded from the others and the main walk. That meant I was the only one who could see the two men in cheap suits waiting for me on my small front porch.

THREE

I FIGURED THEY WERE FEDS. NOT COPS. MIAMI COPS

have a *little* style, whereas these two wore black and gray off-the-rack suits, white shirts, narrow ties with no pattern. The one on the right had his jacket off, folded over his arm, his underarms already darkening with perspiration. He had dark hair, cut short. Black wraparound sunglasses. The one on the left, in the gray suit, squinted to beat the sun, his hair light brown and starting to thin. I put them at thirty, maybe thirty-five.

"Gregg Pulaski?" Gray Suit asked as I approached. He only pronounced two of the Gs.

I nodded.

"I'm Special Agent O'Connor. This is Special Agent Costa, with the Federal Bureau of Investigation."

Nailed it.

"Wondering if we could have a moment of your time," Costa said. His voice was gruff, like he needed to clear his throat. But he didn't.

"Mind if I see some identification?" I asked. I had no doubts they were legit—who would get off faking being a fed?!?!—but FBI agents sort of rubbed me the wrong way, and I was feeling a little catty.

I watched their faces. O'Connor smiled, but it seemed forced. Costa showed no expression as they both provided badges, which I scrutinized ever so briefly. Timothy O'Connor and Tom Costa—were indeed G-men.

"How'd you know where to find me?" I asked.

"A Ms. . . . . Miss? . . . Dawson said you would likely be here. Said since she hadn't heard from you—Thanks," he said, pocketing his badge as I returned it. "Said you were probably still asleep, so when you didn't answer, we decided to wait a few minutes and try again."

Point, Dawson. I would check in with her as soon as I was done with the fibbies.

"Would you like to come in?" I asked.

They nodded, and I let them into my villa. A little over a thousand square feet, it wasn't huge, but more than sufficient for a bachelor. I took a step to the right, into the kitchen, but nodded at the living room, down three steps. "Have a seat. Can I offer either of you something to drink?"

They declined as programed, and I opened the fridge and poured myself a glass of pulp-free orange juice. While I had the door open, I pulled Gia's sunglasses from my shirt pocket and flipped them onto the top shelf, where no one would ever see them in my possession. I spent just a moment wondering about a brother who would mar such a lovely face by buying them for his sister, then shut the door and joined Costa and O'Connor.

They had taken seats on my couch, and I pulled an old rocker away from the wall and sat down. I sipped my orange juice. "What's on your mind?"

"Mr. Pulaski," O'Connor began, "we are aware of your role here."

We made eye contact, and I knew which role he meant. What I didn't know is if he'd leveled that as some sort of threat. His face belied it if so.

"We're hoping that, in that role, you can help us out."

"How so?" I asked before taking another drink. To throw off their rhythm, I said, "Are you sure I can't get you something to drink?"

"We're sure," Costa said.

I nodded.

"How familiar are you with the guest list this weekend?" O'Connor asked.

"I've met a few of them, but not very."

He nodded at Costa, who whipped a manila folder out from under his arm and jacket. He handed it to O'Connor who handed it to me, only after I confirmed it didn't have sweat spots on it.

"What's this?"

O'Connor nodded for me to open it, which I did. I was looking at a photograph of a man in his seventies—weathered skin, a thinning but full head of wavy white hair, and deep-set brown eyes covered by eyebrows that could serve as toupées if the hair fully thinned. He wore a light blue shirt with a crisp, white collar, a gold chain visible under it. His face was stern, but looked intentionally so, as if a charming old guy was trying to look mean.

"That's Angelo Ravello," O'Connor said, "former head of the Ravello Crime Family in Long Island."

"Name's vaguely familiar," I said. I looked up. "He's here?"

"Checked in last night. Traveling with two of his grandkids."

I took another drink to try to cover any expression. I supposed it was possible multiple old men had checked into The Grandeur with their grandkids—just like it was possible Gia had left out that her grandfather was a former mafia don.

"You looking to bust him for something?"

"He's clean."

"For now," Costa muttered.

"Check out the other photos," O'Connor said. I shuffled through three more, all old guys with sparse hair and long ears. O'Connor identified them as Francesco Romano, former consigliere for the Ravello family; Niccolo Marino, retired don from Cincinnati; and Vincenzo De Luca, one-time underboss in Minneapolis. All had reservations and had been confirmed to have arrived at The Grandeur.

"I take it that's not coincidence," I said, closing the folder and handing it back to Costa.

He shook his head and sat back, smoothing his tie. "Keep it."

I withdrew the folder.

"It's not," O'Connor said. "Allegedly, they're all here on vacation to swap stories and relive the good old days."

"You suspect something else?"

"The Bureau is suspicious by nature, especially of the mob," O'Connor said. "Miami being what it is, and the resort's reputation being what it is, we're more suspicious."

I drained my juice without taking offense. With its combination of luxury and exclusivity in an international hub like Miami, The Grandeur had become an enclave for white-collar criminals and covert operatives. They could meet in anonymity, conducting their business off the radar. It was one of the reasons I was employed.

"We also have credible rumors from a mole within the Ravello family that some sort of deal is in the works."

"Something's going down this weekend," Costa said.

"I thought you said all these guys are retired."

"Officially they are," O'Connor said. "But no one ever really leaves the Family. They're retired but still calling the shots or working as emissaries for whoever is in charge now. Either way, we think something's going down this weekend, as Tom said, or else the groundwork is being laid this weekend."

"What do you want from me?"

"Do what you do. Keep your ear to the ground, for starters. Obviously, if you have a chance to eavesdrop on any conversations or search their rooms while they're getting the early-bird special for dinner, that would be great."

I didn't tell them that I didn't make a habit of breaking into guests' rooms.

"Ravello's granddaughter's cute," Costa said. "Maybe you can get cozy with her."

"You think a former mafia don brought his granddaughter along on a business trip and spilled the beans to her?"

"Maybe not so overtly," O'Connor said. He sighed, then stood. Costa and I took our cues. "We don't expect miracles, but if you glean anything, pick up any hints . . . we'd love to know about it."

"How should I get in touch with you?" I asked.

"We're in room 309, next door to De Luca."

"Got his wall tapped?" I asked with a smirk.

"We do," Costa said.

"I'll let you know if I find anything," I said, not expecting to and certainly not intending to use my lunch date with Gia to probe her for info about her grandfather's business dealings. But I had to at least keep up appearances with the feds.

"Thanks for your time, Mr. Pulaski," O'Connor said and extended his hand. I shook it, then Costa's, then walked them to the door. I closed it behind them and took a breath. Then I checked my watch. Plenty of time to check in with Summer before lunch with Gia. But first, I went to my bedroom dresser, opened the top drawer, and picked out a new pair of Porsche aviators.

FOUR

SUMMER DAWSON LIVES UP TO HER NAME. SHE WEARS

floral sundresses and flared skirts, draws her wavy brown hair back
with a ribbon or headband or reasonable looking oval sunglasses to
add an unneeded youthful appearance, and smells like citrus thanks
to her Chanel perfume. Summer speaks softly but firmly, and she
greets guests and her staff with a warm smile and jovial blue-green
eyes. Her firm scowl and wintry glare get reserved for me.

The scowl and glare were there when I entered her office, after
announcing myself with a single-knuckle knock on one of the glass
panes in dual French doors that opened from the secretary's office.
Summer looked up from behind a wide desk, cluttered as always.
Behind her, a wide window looked down into the atrium. It was
tinted to provide privacy, which was something Summer craves in all
aspects of life. She looked at me for just a moment, then flitted her

eyes to a clock on the wall, before looking back down at a sheaf of papers on her desk.

"Morning," I said.

"Is it still?"

I grinned, glanced out the windows to my left, her right, through which the Miami skyline was visible over the treetops. Then I pulled out one of two chairs in front of her desk and sat down.

"Have a seat," she said, not looking up. She twiddled a Montblanc pen back and forth between her index and middle finger as she continued to study the papers in front of her, the top few pages held up by her other hand. I can play her games, so I waited. She lifted one more page, scanned for another minute, and then finally gripped her pen in a writing posture and scrawled her name. She dropped the ends of the papers and slid the sheaf forward. She set her pen on top of it and sat back in her ergonomic office chair. She actually smiled. "Sorry to keep you waiting."

I grinned again, well aware she was not sorry but pointing out that someone who keeps someone else waiting ought to be sorry. I let it pass and got down to business. "Busy weekend?"

"About normal. Did the gentlemen from the FBI find you?"

"More like I found them."

"What did they want?"

I was tempted to tell her it was need to know, but she would counter that she needed to know since it was her resort. I'd remind her that it was actually her father's, she'd remind me that he had made her the resort manager, at which point I'd remind her he'd made me Head Security Officer, and she'd scrunch up her button nose and make some comment about poor decisions. I decided to save us both the time and trouble. Plus she probably already knew and was just testing me.

"They think retired mobsters are cooking something up this weekend."

"Cooking what?"

"They have no idea."

"What did they want you to do?"

"Eavesdrop and snoop."

Summer didn't reply, but her expression said I was aptly suited for just such a task. I knew that, because she'd actually said it with the same expression before.

"Anything else going on?" she asked.

I briefly mentioned Diana Berglowe. I didn't say anything about my conversation or lunch plans with Gia, nor about her being related to one of the aforementioned mobsters. Not that Summer wouldn't likely find out all the above. She has a knack for knowing everything that happens at the resort.

"I have something for you to look into," she said, lifting a manila folder from a rack on her right. She handed it to me, and I opened it to see several computer printouts showing numbers and dollar figures and looking far too complicated for what was practically the weekend.

"What is this?" I asked.

"We've experienced a couple thefts in recent days. That is a report of inventory and sales that shows the discrepancy."

"I would have believed you," I said, looking up from the numbers. "What's being stolen?"

"Fudge."

My eyes froze. "Fudge?"

"And taffy. Some cookies."

"You're serious?"

"Yes."

"You catch any guests taking the rest of their bar soap home with them too?"

Sometimes there's a good reason she glares at me.

"We keep meticulous records of inventory, including breakage and spoilage. Likewise with our sales records. And it's not a mere piece or two. Several pounds of taffy have gone missing the last two days, and twice that amount of fudge."

"You think someone on staff has been snacking on duty?" I asked somewhat tongue-in-cheek, albeit with a suspect already in mind.

"That is what I want our Head Security Officer to find out."

"You actually have someone count pieces of taffy every night?"

"Of course not. Servers estimate as they restock, and we compare that to sales nightly and weekly, as evidenced in the printout I gave you."

I lowered my eyes to accept my scolding.

"If this was one or two pieces, we wouldn't notice and wouldn't make a deal if we did. But, like I said, this is something larger, and I want to nip it in the bud."

I nodded.

"You don't agree?"

"I think it's small change, but you're the boss."

"I'm having lunch with Collins," she said, "but I'll be back by mid-afternoon. You'll keep me apprised?"

I nodded again.

"What's that?"

"What's what?"

"That smirk."

"Was I smirking?"

"You still are."

I shrugged.

"What?" she asked, still soft, but very firm.

"I can't help notice how you mention Collins in every one of our conversations."

"He *is* my fiancé."

I nodded.

"What now?"

"I just don't see why you have to keep reminding me he's your fiancé."

"I'm not reminding you of anything. He's the most important person in my life, so it's only natural he will come up in conversation."

I nodded once more, and it incurred more glaring, but no further questioning. She did say, "I have some things to take care of."

"Enjoy your lunch," I said as I stood.

It was her turn to smirk, and I had no doubt she knew the details of my lunch plans by the way she said, "You too."

FIVE

SWEET CREAMS PARLOR & CONFECTIONARY IS CONVEN-

iently located between the pool deck and the resort's beach access. Open from ten until ten daily, it serves a dozen flavors of ice cream, twice that many types of taffy, several varieties of fudge, cookies and cupcakes, and a wide assortment of candy, along with malts, shakes, sodas, snow cones, and coffees. With booths, tables, and counter seating looking out the windows, plus several outdoor tables, the parlor has enough seating to keep up with the influx of patrons that starts mid-afternoon and lasts some days until closing time. A few minutes after eleven a.m., it's usually pretty empty, and this was no exception. A couple at one of the outdoor tables and two women in a booth on the right were the only customers when I entered. As expected, Brooke Finnegan was behind the counter.

"Hi, Shades," she called out. She wore a blue Sweet Creams T-shirt, her blond hair piled up on top of a matching visor. Unlike

Summer, she greeted me with a smile, one that was hard not to return. Brooke's a cute kid—and I mean that, she's eighteen, enrolling at the University of Miami (nobody's perfect) in the fall. But the cherubic smile that usually graces her face seems to be a natural outflow of her personality—good-natured, upbeat, easy to talk to. And before you think it, Brooke's like a sister to me.

"Hey, Brooke," I said as I slid off my sunglasses and tucked them in my pocket. I approached the service counter, which displayed all the treats the parlor had to offer. "You have rocky road today?"

"Won't it spoil your lunch?" she asked with a cockeyed look.

"I'll come back later," I said, then peered through the display case myself.

"What brings you in here so early?" she asked.

"Summer," I said.

The perpetual smile faded a little.

I made sure no one was eavesdropping, then said, "She told me someone's been stealing from the parlor."

Brooke nodded.

"What's the end of day procedure?" I asked, nodding at the trays of fudge under glass to the left.

"We rotate out any expired product, put some things back in the cooler. The rest is left in the display cases, and they're locked."

"So someone would have had to smash and grab, which would have left evidence, or else stolen a key."

"And all the keys are locked in the box in the back room."

"Who has a key to the key box?"

"All employees who have a master key."

"You?"

Her mouth opened.

"I'm not insinuating, Brooke."

(I was.)

She closed her mouth and swallowed. "Yes, I have a key."

"You lose it or misplace it?"

She shook her head.

"Hear anyone else say they had?"

"No."

"So since none of the glass has been broken, and nobody lost a key . . . Either an employee decided to take some goodies home one night, or a customer pilched them during the day. Any idea who or how?"

Brooke shrugged. "It's all out in the open, so to speak anyhow. When it gets busy . . ."

Her point was made. I'd never seen more than three people staffing the parlor at once, and when customers were backed up and complaining about flavor availability, tables needed to be wiped down, and some little tyke hadn't quite made it to the bathroom and had peed in the hallway . . . well, somebody swiping some creamsicle taffy or marshmallow almond fudge was easy to understand. I wasn't too concerned, despite Summer's desire to nip the theft in the bud.

"Keep your eyes and ears open?"

"I will."

"You working all weekend?"

"Afraid so."

"It's good money," I said, aware that Brooke was trying to save away tuition money.

She dipped her head.

"Want me to put in with Summer for a raise?"

"Like you have that power."

We both grinned, then she dealt with a customer who took a waffle cone of mint chocolate chip to go. After quickly wiping down the counter, Brooke came back to where I was eyeing the fudge. She leaned on the counter. "Any VIPs here this week?"

I smiled. Brooke, like any eighteen-year-old girl, I suppose, was prone to being starstruck. Last February, Tom Cruise had been rumored to be staying in the penthouse, and it was all anyone could think of—might he be up there dancing in his underwear before stopping in for a martini or a steak or a double scoop of cookies 'n cream. I, of course, am immune to being starstruck . . . unless Stefanie Powers was to drop in for the weekend . . .

"Not that I'm aware of," I answered, then followed up with *my* usual question for her. "Any unusual characters stop in?" It was as good of a question for anyone at The Grandeur as it was for Brooke. You never know in customer service what sort of interaction you might be in for.

She wrinkled her nose. "I had a couple old guys in here not half an hour ago. Three of them in fact. They were like an old married couple—well, triple I guess," she said with a giggle.

I raised an eyebrow.

"Bickering and grumbling at each other, but goodhearted I think."

"Not distracting you while they swiped watermelon taffy, were they?"

She laughed quietly, more of a smile really. "No. They were arguing about who made better linguini, and then reliving some football game."

"A football game?"

"The Vikings and . . . it must have been the Dolphins because I heard them mention Marino. Dan Marino is the Dolphins' quarterback, isn't he?"

I nodded, my mind drifting to my conversation with Agents Costa and O'Connor, about some old mobsters, one of whom was named Marino and another of whom was from Minneapolis, home of the NFL's Minnesota Vikings. And which mobster didn't love linguini?

"Did I say something wrong?" she asked.

"No. They say anything else interesting?"

"Not really. Took them a while to figure out what ice cream to get and who was paying. Oh, they kept talking about how they were going to score this weekend. I thought they were still talking football, but I got the feeling it was something else."

"They didn't say what?"

Brooke fiddled with her updo, thinking for a moment. Then she shook her head. "I can't recall anything specific. Why? Are they VIPs of some kind?"

I shrugged. "Beats me."

The bell over the door tinkled, and a family with teenagers made a beeline for the ice cream. I said goodbye to Brooke and left her to her work, then headed back out into what was turning into a very warm midday, wondering both if I had done enough investigating the thefts to satisfy Summer and how I could do enough investigating of the mob to satisfy Costa and O'Connor.

SIX

Gia was sitting very near where Diana Berglowe had

been at the Circle Bar when I arrived just before twelve-thirty. She had changed, obviously, into a red and white striped top, tied in a knot around the waist, white pants, heeled sandals, and the same straw hat. It worked equally well with her casual lunch attire as it had with her swimwear, and perhaps explained why she wasn't wearing the sunglasses I'd given her. She smiled when she saw me, nudged away a tray of peanuts that had been at arm's length, and deposited the last nut from her hand into her mouth.

"You came," she said, sliding off her stool.

"You doubted?"

From under her hat, an eyebrow rose. "I saw you chatting with another woman after you left me, and I thought perhaps you'd had a better offer."

I looked at her for a second, wondering if I detected jealousy or banter. I wasn't sure, and opted to diffuse. "A guest who wanted to speak with me in my official capacity. Nothing more."

Never mind the hand holding and deep looks into the eyes.

Gia winked. "I wasn't too worried. She didn't have a hat."

I grinned as I offered her my arm, and we strolled away from the bar and toward the live oak. It was over fifty feet tall, its thick, low limbs draped with Spanish moss extending over the walkways more than half its height from a four-foot-thick trunk. Somehow, someone affiliated with the resort had determined it was over 150 years old, and it had been carefully preserved during the hotel's construction. I mentioned this to Gia as we strolled under the shade of its boughs, and she paused to look up at the filtered light trickling through the foliage. I'd marveled at said light before, especially early in the morning or late in the evening, and instead turned my attention to the way the breeze took curls of Gia's hair and drew them away from round cheeks.

She caught me looking, and I covered by nodding onward.

"Where are we going?" she asked.

"Only place open for lunch on a weekday is The Coconut Grille."

"Sounds exotic."

I shrugged. "They have a small menu of burgers and sandwiches every day, a few rotating hot options, a salad and soup bar. Patio seating."

"Works for me."

As we walked, I determined Gia had found her way to the pool deck but hadn't explored the rest of the grounds since arriving the night before. So I gave her the brief layout, stopping as we reached the entrance to the building housing both The Coconut Grille and the more formal, dinner-only Oak Room. The Coconut Grille was mostly full, but we ordered the Coco Club for me and the salad bar for her and found a table on the patio next to and partially in the shade of a thirty-foot-tall silver palm.

"So, Gia," I said as she was tossing her salad. I picked up a couple fries. "Is that short for something?"

"Giovanna," she said.

"Italian."

"You say that as if you're not surprised."

"You said your brother's name was Tony." I shrugged and lifted a quarter of my sandwich. "I took a shot."

Gia looked at me for a moment, as if trying to see past a veneer, then stabbed into her lettuce. I enjoyed a few bites of my club. Summer is young, and there has been more than a little muttering about someone so young being named manager of an entire resort by her "daddy." There's also muttering that he actually helps run things from behind the scene. Whatever the case, for all the flak I have to take from her (and give in return) she does a good job, including hiring great chefs. I've never had a bad meal at The Oak Room or The Coconut Grille, and I've tried almost everything on their respective menus.

"How does one become a hotel detective?" Gia asked after dabbing nothing on the corner of her mouth with her napkin.

"One gets discharged from the Navy but has a really good relationship with his old C.O.," I said. That was more or less a version of the truth.

"Why were you discharged from the Navy?"

"They have this thing about sailors not squinting or shielding their eyes whenever it's sunny."

"You really are sensitive to sunlight."

I nodded.

"I mean, I thought you were just saying it casually. But it's an actual medical condition?"

"It's called photophobia."

"Is it serious?"

"I have a mild-ish case of it, but serious enough for the Navy."

"I'm sorry," she said, then looked down at her salad.

"Don't be. My life's worked out pretty well."

She picked at her salad while I polished off the first quarter of the club. I downed a few fries, licked the seasoning off my fingers, and reached for my iced tea. "Something wrong?" I asked before taking a drink.

"Can I ask you a sort of personal question?"

"You mean more personal than my career and medical history?" I grinned. "Go for it."

"Are the sunglasses you wear terribly expensive?"

I was facing north, and a palm frond shielded the side of my face. Having acclimated to the outdoors, I lowered my shades and only had to squint a fraction. "Yes," I said.

She nodded.

"Why?"

"Because someone stole the pair you gave me."

I frowned.

"I took a brief swim after we talked, maybe fifteen minutes, and when I came back to my chair, they were gone. I'd laid them on top of my hat, next to my towel, and somebody swiped them. If they're expensive, I guess that explains it."

I was distracted by the thought of Diana Berglowe's fear that there was a thief on the grounds, and by the fact that Summer had tasked me with finding one. Then again, pearls, Porsche sunglasses, and candy were an odd combo for a single thief to target. All such thoughts were chased away by anger that somebody had targeted Gia while she was swimming. And, technically, on my watch.

"I can get you another pair," I said.

Her eyes widened. "You already gave me one." She traced the brim of her hat. "This works for now."

"I told Summer—my boss—that we should put up a closed-circuit security camera or two over the patio, but she thought people might not like swimming in front of a camera."

Gia made a face as she shook her head.

I shrugged. "It's not like you're not in front of a bunch of people already."

"A camera's somehow different."

"Probably wouldn't have gotten enough to ID the perp anyhow."

"I'm sorry," she said, spontaneously reaching out a hand and putting it on mine. It was a quick gesture, immediately withdrawn, and we went back to eating. We resumed light chatter. I asked where she was from, even though I knew it was Long Island, home of the Ravello Family. She asked if I had always lived in Florida, and I said I had, except for my time aboard a United States Navy aircraft carrier. Then she asked me about my ring.

I wiped fry seasoning and breadcrumbs off my fingers and slid the ring off my right ring finger. She swallowed, dabbed her bare lip, and wiped off her hands. I extended it to her.

"Seventy-four?" she asked.

"Nineteen seventy-four. We were Class 4A state champs, football."

"We?"

"Leon High, in Tallahassee."

"Seventy-four," she said, fingering the ring. "Ten years ago."

"I was a freshman, a gunner on special teams, mostly."

She was about to say something when a gravelly voice shouted out, "Giovanna!"

Gia turned her head to the doors leading inside from the patio, where two old men had just emerged. The one on the right carried two drink cups, and the one on the left a tray with two plates. He had wavy white hair, extra-thick eyebrows, and jovial smile. I recognized him as Angelo Ravello, Gia's grandfather, and former head of the Ravello Crime Family. The man beside him was one of the other three for whom Costa and O'Connor had shown me files, but I couldn't recall which. He was several inches taller, thinner and bonier, with less hair on top of his head and just as much over his eyes. His skin was like leather, and I saw too much of it because he wore shorts with tall white socks and sandals. A big nose and a big grin filled his face.

Gia's matched it as she jumped up, still holding my ring. "Uncle Frankie!"

They moved to embrace, then he realized he was about to slosh diet soda on her blouse. He carefully balanced the cups on Angelo's tray, then turned and hugged Gia. "How are you, bunny?" They kissed cheeks, he pinched hers, she traced his. Then she stepped back, straightening her hat.

"Goodness," he said, "I haven't seen you since . . ."

"Reno," she said.

"Reno, nineteen . . ."

"Seventy-seven?"

"Seventy-eight," Angelo said from beside her. "Hello, *mia perla.*"

"Hello, Grandpa." She turned, as if remembering me. "Oh, this is, um—"

"You don't know who you're having lunch with?" Frankie asked.

I slid back from the table. "Gregg Pulaski," I said, "but my friends call me Shades."

"Angelo Ravello." He made to shake my hand, but realized he held the tray.

"Allow me," I said, carefully taking it from him. I then shook a wrinkled but firm hand. Frankie's a moment later was like a vice grips.

"Oh, your ring," Gia said, suddenly handing it back.

"Class ring," I said, holding it up briefly, lest they get any sort of ideas. I slid it back on. "You're welcome to join us," I added, thinking how proud the two fibbies would be of me.

They both looked dumbfounded for a moment, even exchanging glances, before Angelo made eye contact with his nodding granddaughter. "Vinny and Nicky are coming too."

"Nicky had to pee," Frankie muttered.

"He always has to," Angelo said. "You remember Vincenzo and Niccolo, Gia?"

"Reno?"

He nodded.

"The anniversary that never was?"

Angelo nodded again with a smile.

"We can make room," she said.

I nodded.

"Naw. You two enjoy your lunch," he said, offering me another handshake. Thus so did Frankie, and I mentally scheduled an X-ray for the afternoon. He gave Gia another nip on the cheek with a promise to see her later, then they took their cups and tray and set out to find a table on the other side of the patio. We sat back down.

"Sorry," Gia said.

"Nothing to be sorry for," I said, putting my sunglasses back on.

"Frankie and Grandpa Angie used to work together," she said, and I wondered from her tone if she knew what line of work that was. I shrugged it off for the time being and went back to work on my club, keeping an eye out for Vincenzo De Luca and Niccolo Marino. I recognized both of them when they exited and turned left on the patio, each carrying their own tray and drink for what it was worth.

We talked a little more as we finished eating. Gia was a waitress back on Long Island, at a little family-owned pizza place. I probed a little, trying to find out just how deep the Family had hooks into the restaurant, and in turn learned Gia's dream was to be a chef. And she probed a little, for her own reasons, and found out why I joined the Navy and not the Army or Air Force. But that's a story for a different day.

"So, I should check in with my boss," I said as we were standing to leave. "Can I walk you back to your suite or wherever you're headed?"

"I'd like that," she said.

We turned to go back inside, when Angelo called out from a few tables over and signaled for us to come over. Gia looked at me, and I gave a subtle nod and followed her. Angelo re-introduced his granddaughter to Vincenzo and Niccolo, then looked at me. "And this is Gregg Pulaski?" he asked, looking for confirmation. I gave it with a nod.

"That's not Italian," Niccolo practically growled.

Angelo waved him off before I could answer. "Gregg, you play any poker?"

"Yeah."

"We're looking for a fifth for a game tonight. You interested?"

Poker with a bunch of former mobsters? What could go wrong? Then again, Costa and O'Connor would have to give me credit for doing my due diligence—and maybe even foot the bill. "Yeah, why not?"

Angelo clapped his hands. "Great."

"But, I told you, my friends call me Shades, and I only play with friends."

"Shades, huh?" Vincenzo asked, his voice high and strained. He pointed a somewhat gnarled finger at my sunglasses. "You can't read markings on the cards with those or something, can you?"

"You planning on marking the cards?" I asked with a grin, and he pointed some more and cackled in laughter in response.

"About nine o'clock," Angelo said. "We've reserved the card room in the clubhouse. You know where that is?"

"I do. Nine o'clock."

He offered a hand, and I shook it, then waved to the rest of the guys as we turned to leave. Once inside, Gia grabbed my arm and leaned in to whisper. "I hope you know what you're doing."

"What do you mean?"

"I mean, I love my grandpa and Uncle Frankie, but they start smoking and drinking and, well . . ." She looked up at me. "I'm afraid you'll lose your shorts."

"Don't worry," I said. "I keep an extra pair of those too."

SEVEN

FROM THE DINING CENTER IT'S ONLY A SHORT WALK BACK

to the side entrance to the hotel atrium, but Gia and I took our time. The atrium is 125 feet in diameter, two stories tall, with a couple dozen palm trees and twice that many fern bushes providing seclusion for seating areas, for bar patrons, those waiting for their parties, or anyone looking for an interior place to read a book or relax. There's also a ten-foot-high, 6,000-gallon aquarium behind the check-in counter, and we stopped for a moment so Gia could marvel at the more than twenty species of fish that swim through its artificial reefs and kelp. I cast my eyes up toward Summer's window, even though I couldn't see through it, then watched Gia watch the fish.

She and her brother were sharing a two-bedroom suite on the seventh floor, next to Angelo's suite. So, after she gawked at the marine life for a few minutes, we headed for the elevators just outside the atrium.

"I never did thank you for lunch," she said as we waited for one of the trio of elevators' doors to open.

"Yes you did, right when I paid."

"I meant more formally."

"Well, you're welcome."

"And to think, if Tony hadn't bought me this hat," she said lifting her eyes to it.

The elevator dinged, a couple got out, and we got in. I pressed the 7. "What do you have in mind for the rest of your stay?"

"I don't know. This was sort of last minute, so I didn't plan too much."

The doors closed and we began to ascend.

"What do you do for fun back on Long Island?"

"Sailing on the sound, horseback riding on the beach, I play tennis."

"You do?"

She nodded.

"We have two of the only grass courts in southern Florida."

"You have grass courts?"

I nodded.

"How do you manage that in all this heat?"

"Not easily. Our grounds crew's top-notch."

Gia bit her lip. "I didn't bring a racquet, and I have . . ."

I had started smiling, and the doors dinged on the seventh floor.

"Let me guess, you play tennis," she said.

I gestured for her to exit the elevator, then followed her. "I do."

"And you have a spare racquet?"

"I could probably scare one up."

Gia licked her lips. "Are you any good?"

"Not bad."

"Because I don't want to chase stray balls around. I play to win."

"I play not to lose, which makes for long matches sometimes, but I can hold my own."

"We'll see about that." She stopped in front of room 709, which I briefly noted was exactly four floors above Agents Costa and O'Connor, not that it mattered in the least. "Want to see the view?"

"Sure, I never get to see the Miami skyline."

She whacked my arm and I grinned, both on cue. Then I followed her into the suite, the layout of which was familiar. Living room straight ahead, kitchenette around a closet to the right, bedrooms on either side, each with their own full bath. French doors opened onto a balcony that was also accessible from both bedrooms. Everything was decorated in whites and pastels—soft oranges and blues and purples and pinks, very Miami. Of course, the artwork had a nautical theme.

"Tony," she called out, as I swung the door shut. It thumped twice, and we looked at each other. There was a third thump, this one coming from the bedroom on the right.

"That's my room," Gia said. Before I could stop her, she took another step. "Tony?"

Taking only a moment to remove her hat and flop it over the couch, she strode toward the ajar door to her right. I was right behind her as she grabbed the knob, swung it inward, and screamed.

I jumped beside her, bumping her to the side and sort of behind me. The room was empty, save for the usual hotel furniture—bed, nightstand, dressing table, dresser with a TV on it. Like in the living room, paned French doors opened to the balcony. One of them was ajar.

I looked back to Gia. "Was someone in here?"

"I saw a body move past the window."

"Wait here," I said. I dashed around the bed and burst out onto the balcony. There was no one there. Neither set of doors was open. I turned behind me and looked at the slatted wall that separated Gia and Tony's balcony from the next suite's over. It was six-feet tall, so I ran to the railing and peeked my head around. Nothing but rattan furniture and closed doors. I hurried to the other end of the balcony and peeked around that wall and saw the same thing. I turned my eyes down, wondering if the body Gia had seen could have swung over the side and down a story. Theoretically, but unless it had been a professional cat burglar, he or she would have been more likely to fall seven stories to their death or permanent paralysis.

I retraced my steps and entered through the doors into Gia's bedroom. She stood unmoved.

"Did you see anyone?"

I shook my head, told her to wait again, and hurried out into the hallway. Suite 709 was more or less in the middle of the hallway. If somebody had swung from one balcony to the next—a slightly less suicidal move than dropping down a floor—and entered an adjacent room, I doubted they could have exited the room into the hallway and made it to either end without me seeing them. If it was me, and the adjacent room was empty, I'd wait a few minutes, expecting to be looked for in the hallway. I'd maybe even find a pair of swim trunks, if there were any in the room, don them and drape a towel around my neck and casually head out.

On second thought, scratch that. Not wearing another dude's swim trunks. But you get the idea.

So I waited two minutes, until Gia opened the door. "Anything?" she asked.

"No," I said, and followed her back into the room. "You're sure you saw somebody?"

"Positive. And I didn't leave the door ajar."

"Could you see anything about them? Man or woman? Hair? Clothes?"

She shook her head to all. "It was just a blur."

"Well, they're gone now."

"Why would somebody break into my room?"

"They realized what a mistake they'd made not taking the hat earlier."

"Don't be funny."

I shrugged. And didn't say, "You're a former Mafia don's granddaughter, you tell me." Instead, I said it could be random, someone looking for the high-end items (like pearl necklaces) that top-floor travelers might have on them. I also asked, because it was a reasonable question given events, if she could think of any reason anyone might be targeting her or her brother.

"No. It's not like we were flaunting jewelry or anything at the airport."

Someone had taken my sunglasses from her, but while they were expensive, they weren't *that* expensive. I promised I would investigate it further, and started by searching all the doors and windows for any signs of a break-in. There were none, meaning the intruder either had palmed a keycard from a maid or was a pro. I then offered to stay until Tony returned from golfing or Angelo from wherever he and his fellow mobsters were hanging out. But Gia's color had returned, and she seemed to be all right. She declined, saying she wanted to try to take a nap, what with her needing energy to play tennis later. I took that as a good sign and said I'd call her once I made a reservation for one of the courts. I made sure she locked all the doors, and then went to see if Summer had returned from her lunch date to let her know we had a real thief—or at least, a would-be thief—on the premises.

And to track down Kevin and borrow his tennis racquet.

EIGHT

I WAS IN REAL TROUBLE.

Summer had not yet been back from lunch, so I had bypassed her and checked in with Lenny, the Chief of Security. He'd let me look at the security footage from the cameras at the east end of the seventh-floor hallway and overlooking the elevators on the seventh floor. Since I'd exited Gia's room, nobody had left either adjacent room. Tony had returned, dressed very much like a preppy golfer. Several other guests had left their rooms, two of which had been odd-numbered rooms on the south side, like Gia and Tony's. But I didn't think a middle-aged woman in a jumper was a likely candidate, and the younger woman in shorts, a tank top, and flip-flops had been several rooms away, meaning she would have had to hop from balcony to balcony. I was left to conclude that the person Gia had seen was either a figment of her imagination (and her door hadn't been properly closed and had slipped ajar), a ninja, or still in an adjacent room.

I asked Lenny to check the footage again later that evening and let me know if anyone in the least bit suspicious exited one of the southern rooms on the seventh floor. Not yet ready to go door-to-door looking for a person I couldn't identify anyhow, and doubting it was prudent to let Diana know her concerns seemed valid without having any way to reassure her that I was making progress, I'd turned my attention to tennis. Hence my trouble.

I'm a pretty good athlete, and I play a fair amount of tennis. And, while not a chauvinist, I recognize that men are usually bigger, stronger, and faster than women—Billie Jean King beating a man old enough to be her father aside—and thus figured I'd overwhelm Gia if I brought my "A" game. So I backed off on my serve in the first set, only to have her rip numerous forehand winners down the line. She also kept me off balance with her serve, and, in part because my three-quarter effort on serving bled into the rest of my game, broke me at 2-1 and held serve to win the first set 6-3.

It was a spectacular afternoon, hot but with a breeze that hinted—as did billowing clouds—at late afternoon thundershowers. And the courts at The Grandeur are indeed pristine, surrounded on either end by eight-foot-tall hedges and on either side of the dual courts by poplar trees and palms. It's like playing tennis in a garden, which is sort of the idea—ask the folks at Wimbledon. Plus Gia looked cute as the dickens in a tennis dress she had apparently purchased at the gift shop. So I didn't mind losing, except that I hate losing. And for our side wager.

I started rolling in the second set, now serving like a man. But Gia held serve, and we were tied 3-3 when a pair of double faults put me in a Love-30 hole. If I went down another break, I didn't like my chances of coming back. So I took a moment to compose myself, wiping sweat from my forehead on my left arm's sweatband. Then I looked at Gia, waiting at the baseline of the deuce court.

She had emerged from the women's locker room in the clubhouse, catching my attention in the dress and then suggesting we make the match a little more interesting.

"How's that?" I had asked.

"If I win, you have to take me to the best restaurant in Miami for dinner tomorrow."

"Tomorrow?" I said, still taking in the dress.

"Grandpa Angie insisted on having dinner with Tony and me tonight."

"Okay, tomorrow. You tell either of them about what happened?"

She shook her head. "Nothing was taken, and I don't want them to worry."

"They the worrying type?"

"Grandpa Angie for sure. He wouldn't want anything to happen to his little *perla*."

Something about that statement bothered me, but I couldn't place it. And I had more important matters on my mind. "You win, dinner tomorrow. What if I win?"

"*If* you win, you have to take me to the best grocery store in Miami, and I'll make you dinner in your villa tomorrow. Fettuccine Carbonara."

Maybe that was part of the reason I was struggling to return serve—I couldn't get out of my head the picture of Gia in my kitchen, hair in wisps beside her cheeks, a glass of wine in one hand and a spoon in the other testing her sauce while I dug through my closet for a pair of long-stem candles. Not that taking her to Versailles or Joe's Stone Crab was a bad consolation prize, but there's something about having a beautiful woman cook for you, especially in your pad.

I smoked an ace down the T-line, then won a long rally with a delicately placed drop shot, and, once out of danger, went on to win the game easily. I broke at 5 all, then held serve to tie the match at a set apiece. We met at the bench to towel off and slug water. Between deep breaths, I looked at Gia, still cute as the dickens despite perspiring greatly. "I think we should skip the third set and go straight to a tiebreak."

"Why's that?" she asked, then took a quick squirt of water. "Scared you won't get lucky again?"

"Lucky, huh?"

"My backhand let me down."

"I see. No. I don't think we'll get it in." I turned my head up to the clouds, which had stopped billowing and were now towering. They were about to block out the sun.

"Okay," she said.

I emptied my pockets of extra balls and turned to go back to my side of the court. Tennis tiebreakers ditch the unorthodox love-15-30-40 scoring method and are played to seven by ones, with a rule that a player has to win by two. Gia and I were tied 4-4 when the skies opened. Grass courts get awfully slick when wet, and south Florida isn't known for brief, light sprinkles in the afternoon. So we quickly gathered our gear and headed to the clubhouse. On the off chance the rain abated quickly, we stood outside on the north portico. After a minute of listening to the rain, I caught Gia looking at me.

"I just don't know many guys who play football and tennis," she said.

"I was pretty good at basketball too, until I stopped growing."

"When was that?"

"High school."

"What do your parents do?"

"Do? For a living?"

"Um-hmm."

"Dad's a retired Army colonel who now manages a boutique commercial real estate company and Mom is a mortgage officer at a bank."

"Here in Miami?"

"Tallahassee."

"Hmm."

I squinted at her for a moment, wondering why she was asking. But I reciprocated.

"My father was a dirty rotten bum, or so my mom tells me. I don't remember much of him. They split when I was six."

"I'm sorry."

"So I was raised by a single mom, a grandpa, a host of aunts and uncles, and a two-year-older brother who went from eight to eighteen overnight." She looked my way and smiled. "And I wouldn't change any of it."

"Who taught you to play tennis?"

"Irina Lapidus, a second-generation Russian-American who charges wealthy Long Island families an exorbitant rate to coach their children."

I was eighty percent sure she was telling the truth, and smiled. Well, maybe seventy percent.

Then lightning flashed, thunder cracked almost instantly, and Gia jumped a good couple inches.

"I think the match is suspended indefinitely," I said.

"I think so."

We shook hands, which she initiated, and then went our separate ways to shower and change. The thundershower had moved through by the time we were done, and we agreed to meet for cocktails at the rooftop bar before she, Tony, and Angelo had dinner. I decided, for the sake of my nagging conscience, to check in with Lenny before that, so I walked her back to the atrium, and we parted ways.

Already, I was planning on missing Gia when the Ravello family checked out Sunday.

NINE

By five-thirty when I emerged onto the rooftop

deck, the afternoon thundershowers were nothing more than pink-tinged cumulous clouds on the eastern horizon. Full sunshine had returned, as had the heat. Fortunately, The Grandeur View (the name is corny as heck) rooftop bar features a canopy over the bar area, pergolas covering lounge chairs, umbrellas at the patio-style tables, and planted palms wrapped in twinkling lights. With seating for seventy-five, it's always popular for pre-dinner cocktails and post-dinner relaxation.

Gia was sitting on a rattan sofa under the largest pergola. She turned her head, saw me, smiled, and stood. She wore a knee-length blue sundress, a necklace of polished seashells around her neck. Her hair was drawn back into a ponytail, less alluring but more practical for a rooftop breeze.

"Hey," she said as I approached.

"Hey," I said, continuing the highbrow discourse. "You look nice."

"So do you," she said, fingering my shirtsleeve. I wore the same loafers and white chinos as earlier in the day, but had changed into a thinly-striped garnet and white Winchester shirt. A gold chain to match the Rolex and a new pair of sunglasses, with gold rims and lenses tinged garnet (or a very close approximation thereof), completed the theme. It was lost on most people but was significant to me.

"Any luck on our burglar?" she asked.

I shook my head. Lenny hadn't spotted anything suspicious when I'd checked with him. I concluded that was officially a dead end—however the intruder had escaped, he hadn't been spotted by hotel security cameras, at least not in a way to prove he was the intruder.

"No one else has complained of a burglar?" she asked.

I shook my head again.

"Would you tell me if they had?"

"If you asked."

She sighed. "Shall we get a drink?"

I nodded, reached for her elbow, and led her over to the bar. Most of the stools were taken, so we ordered a pair of margaritas with plans to take them to a seating area in the northeast corner of the roof. The bartender was new, a guy in an orange Hawaiian shirt with the sleeves cut off and spiked blue hair. He fit on the beach, or in some of the more trendy clubs, maybe, but not at a refined resort that catered to exclusive clientele. But, to his credit, he mixed drinks in a hurry.

Gia and I turned to leave and stopped suddenly. "Tony!"

"Gia!"

My eyes widened, taking in what my detective's brain determined was Gia's brother. He had dark hair combed stylishly, tan skin, and decent fashion sense—a light blue blazer over a cream-colored shirt. His face was incredibly relaxed—he was either aloofly casual or stoned. I determined the former; stoners didn't attract women like the one beside him. She had caramel skin and dark black curly hair styled on the side of the top of her head with a bright blue band. Her cocktail dress was black with most colors of the rainbow—including a matching blue—represented in a pattern that swirled across it. She wasn't a working girl, I didn't think, but neither had Tony met her on the golf course.

"Shades, this is by brother, Tony. Tony, Shades."

We shook hands.

"This is Cari," he said, and we both shook hands with her, Gia introducing herself in the process.

"Are you the guy who almost beat my sister in tennis?" Tony asked.

"Three points away when the rain came."

"Just as close to losing," she said.

"Still impressive. Did she tell you she went to State when she was in high school?"

I looked at her.

"Must have slipped my mind."

"We'll have to figure out another way to settle dinner plans," I said.

"Dinner?" Tony asked.

"Tomorrow," Gia said.

"Ah. Well, we're going to grab drinks. Mind if we join you, or are three and four a crowd?"

Gia looked to me.

"Absolutely. We'll save you a couple seats," I said.

"Great."

They went to get the new bartender's attention, and Gia and I scoped out a few pieces of rattan furniture in an alcove enclosed by the backside of the elevator on one side and a four-foot-high "living" fence covered with a variety of plants and flowers adjacent to it. On the other two sides, a half wall was topped with glass and offered views of the Atlantic Ocean straight east and Miami Beach north of the resort property. The sound of the waves, the shrieks and splashes from the pool, and the horns and motors of distant traffic all carried on the breeze. They were muted by rustling palm fronds from a fifteen-foot tree hanging over the seats.

"Any idea who Tony's friend is?" I asked, finally handing Gia's drink to her.

"No. He didn't say anything, but then again, we've barely more than met in the hallway since we got here."

"Hmm."

"Why?"

"It's nothing," I said with a shake of my head. We sat down. Something about Cari bugged me, but I couldn't place it. I get hunches from time to time, whisperings from my subconscious that something is off. I also have little pet peeves that manifest in the same way. As is often the case, I wasn't sure which this was. So I sipped my margarita.

Tony and Cari arrived with a scotch and a pina colada, respectively. He sat next to me and across from Gia, and she beside him on a rattan sofa. She crossed her legs, causing the bottom of her dress to recede, and settled in close to him.

"So, Shades, nickname I assume?" Tony asked.

I nodded.

So did he. "What do you do for a living?" he asked before taking a drink of scotch.

"I'm the Head Security Officer here at the hotel.

"No foolin'?"

"No fooling."

"That's something of a coincidence. I manage security for a chain of mini marts in New York State."

"Quite a responsibility."

"And try getting such a gig with the last name Ravello."

I frowned, as if I had no idea what he meant.

"My grandpa used to run the Ravello Family on Long Island," he said. "Mom married some loser fresh out of college, then divorced him when she caught him with the neighbor chick. Well, she wasn't going to keep his name, so she goes back to being a Ravello, legally switches our names back, and now anywhere we go, Angelo Ravello's name follows us." He took another drink.

"You didn't seem to mind when Angelo Ravello's name brought you to south Florida for the weekend," Gia said.

"Don't get me wrong, I love Gramps," Tony said, crossing his leg onto his knee, revealing he wasn't wearing socks. "But it's taken my entire professional life to prove I'm part of the family but not part of the *Family*."

"We'll air the rest of our dirty laundry on the balcony railing later," Gia said.

He dismissed her with a wave, while beside him Cari snickered.

"How'd you two meet, anyhow?" he asked. "We ran into each other on the beach."

"He come up to you and say he liked your hat?" Gia asked, drawing an odd look from her brother. She sent a quick smirk my way.

"The other way around," Cari said, revealing a Hispanic accent. "I saw him coming out of the water and, I don't know, something came over me and I asked if he'd like to take a walk."

"I told you that weightlifting would pay off, Gia."

"A walk led to an hour in the ice cream parlor during the thunderstorm, and now here."

"I know, she just sees me and walks up to me, and I just say yes to a strange woman," Tony said, looking at me, "but if you saw her in a bikini, would you say no?"

"To-ny," she said, slapping his arm.

"You didn't wear it as repellent, did you?"

She rolled her eyes and took a drink. Then looked at Gia. "So how did you two meet?"

"Oh, yeah," Tony said, dropping his leg and leaning forward.

"It's actually your doing," I said to Tony.

"Oh?" he asked, frowning again.

"He liked the hat you bought me."

"So that's what you meant by the hat crack?"

She nodded.

"You just, what, went up and said you liked her hat?"

"More or less."

"No foolin'?"

I answered with a slight tip of my head, then took a drink.

"Gia, what do you do for a living?" Cari asked.

"She's a junior partner for a major law firm," Tony said, jerking his thumb at Cari. "Worked on that illegals case a few years ago, the ones on the raft from Cuba."

"You mean refugees from Cuba," Gia said.

He dismissed her again.

Gia looked at Cari, then flitted her eyes at Tony before answering, "Well, I used to be a runner for the Ravello Family."

He about choked on his scotch, then spent the next thirty seconds hacking. Then he swore, without apologizing to the ladies afterward.

"It's true, Tony. Before Grandpa retired, I was his private courier."

"Well, you make—" He choke-coughed again, then cleared his throat. "You make it sound like you were a bagman. You were a courier, dropping off baskets of fruit and meat and cheese platters."

"To capos and friendly consiglieres."

"How long has he been retired?" I asked.

"Four years," Tony said. "And he is retired, despite the rumors."

I wasn't sure if that was gospel truth I could take to Costa and O'Connor or Tony Ravello trying to keep his name clear. Gia told Cari that she was now a waitress, and as much for entertainment as to get under her brother's skin, told a few stories about Mafia dealings she had seen take place during her shifts. Then she asked a few questions about the aforementioned Cuban refugees. When the conversation lagged, Cari excused herself to the ladies' room, setting her half-empty glass on the table between all our furniture.

Tony and Gia, meanwhile, engaged in a staring conversation. She blinked first when a palm frond fluttered in a sudden gust of breeze and the sun got in her eyes.

"What happened to your sunglasses?" Tony asked.

Gia looked down.

"What?"

She sighed. "Somebody stole them?"

"Stole them? When?"

"While I was swimming this morning."

"No foolin'?" he said, slower this time. He cut his eyes to me. "You're the Head Security Officer here?"

"That's right."

He pursed his lips for a moment. "Think you could find them?"

"Tony, it's a pair of sunglasses."

"Still, what kind of crud swipes somebody's sunglasses?"

"Somebody might have seen something," I said, "but there's no security cameras overlooking the pool. Best we could do is ask that if anybody saw anything to let us know."

"Maybe we could hang up a few 'Have you seen me?' posters," Gia said.

"Fine, joke about it," Tony said. "It's your eyes." He looked away as he drained his glass, and Gia sent me a raised-eyebrow look. I returned it and took a drink of my own, wondering why Tony seemed so concerned about sunglasses. My hyperactive subconscious was at it again, saying maybe Tony was protesting too much because he was actually part of whatever Angelo Ravello and his cronies were "scoring" this weekend, and maybe the reason he'd given his sister such an ugly pair of sunglasses was so they would stand out, as a signal to someone who was part of the deal. That was how the Mob worked, after all, for dead drops and the like. Or maybe there was a cat burglar at large, one who broke into seventh-floor suites and targeted women's pearls and who also nabbed sunglasses poolside and swiped fudge when cute (in the little sister way) servers weren't looking. Or, and I was leaning this way, maybe Tony Ravello was a little bit of a flake.

When Cari returned, we chatted for another quarter of an hour, and it stayed amicable. Gia was the first to break up the social hour, saying she needed to get ready for dinner. I offered to see her back to her room, more as an excuse to leave than anything, and we said goodbye to Tony and Cari.

We took the stairs since it was only down one level. As we emerged into the hallway, Gia said, "A little of him goes a long way, doesn't it?"

I shrugged.

"You can say it."

"He's got a . . . unique personality."

"That's very diplomatic. Sorry for anything he said that offended you."

"It was fine."

"And please don't spend a second of your time worrying about my—well, I guess your—sunglasses. At least not on my account."

"I won't."

We reached her room and stopped.

"Want me to hang around in case there's a sunglasses thief on the balcony?"

"No, but thanks." She took her keycard from her purse and paused. "You have poker tonight with Grandpa Angie?"

I nodded.

"That'll probably run late. Call me tomorrow morning?"

I nodded again.

"I don't know if we have any plans as a family or not, but at the very least, we can figure out this dinner issue tomorrow."

"I was hoping you'd just volunteer to cook for me."

"You have to earn that," she said with a wink.

"I look forward to it."

"Tomorrow," she said, then slipped inside with a rather demure smile.

TEN

"**So lemme get this straight.**" **Kevin Corrales said.**

"you just walked up to this babe and told her you liked her hat?"

I nodded.

"And it worked?"

"Seems to have. She went to lunch with me, played tennis with me, had a cocktail with me before dinner with her brother and grandpa, and told me to call her in the morning."

"Dang, son."

I flipped the burgers on the charcoal grill on my deck. From where he lay in my hammock, Kevin removed his red and black Atlanta Falcons hat, tousled an unruly mop of black hair, and set the hat back on his head, the brim covering half his face. The hat looked silly with his coral-colored work polo and khaki shorts, both dictated by Summer, but Kevin was the last person to care. He'd started cutting and trimming grass at The Grandeur when he was sixteen, and gradually worked his way up to Head Groundskeeper, a title which made him sound like he worked at a golf course or a Major League ballpark. As lackadaisical and disinterested as Kevin could be about much of life, he was something of a walking dichotomy in that *nobody* worked harder or was more dedicated to his craft than Kevin. Summer couldn't much stand him and his attitude, but had to admit he did good work. It was one of several commonalities that had bonded us as friends.

"You said her brother's a weirdo?" he called from under the cap.

"Not my exact words."

He lifted the brim and looked at me. "What aren't you saying?"

We'd been friends for several years, close enough that he could hear the unspoken. I swallowed. "I don't know, there was something about him, and his lady friend, that I couldn't place but that bugged me."

"Stuff's always bugging you, man."

"I know. And the sunglasses . . ."

"What about 'em?"

"You buy your sister a really nice hat—"

"The kind that makes random dudes come up and hit on her?"

"Yeah. You buy her that hat, and then a cheapo pair of sunglasses?"

"Last thing I bought my sister was a pack of gum."

"I mean if you were a decent, caring human being."

"Maybe he's not. You said he was a weirdo."

"Then why the hat?"

"Shades, man, you're overthinking again." He sat up and spun his feet off the hammock, without it throwing him. It did cause his hat to fall off, so he scratched his head and put it back on. "Those things about done?"

63

"Yeah."

He traipsed back and swung over the deck railing. I grabbed one of two plates sitting on a tray balanced on the corner of the railing and handed it to him. It had two open buns, and I placed a patty on each. Condiments and chips were on a table beside the chair behind me, and he doctored them up with way too much ketchup and slices of American cheese. He grabbed a longneck bottle of Corona and sat down. I loaded burgers on my two buns, went with cheese and mayo, and retrieved my half-empty glass of iced tea from the railing. Instead of sitting, I leaned on the railing and faced him.

"There's just a lot of weird stuff going on today," I said.

"Besides a hot chick like that falling for your 'cute hat' line?"

"Besides that."

"And you eating mayo on a burger. That's disgusting, son."

"You put sour cream and onion potato chips on a PB&J and want to talk disgusting?"

"What else?" he asked before biting a hunk out of his burger.

"Besides the break-in to her suite on the seventh floor by someone who seemed to disappear afterward, there's the middle-aged lady afraid someone wants to steal her pearl necklace, and then Summer's got a bee in her bonnet about fudge and taffy missing from Sweet Creams."

He perked up slightly. "Missing fudge and taffy?"

"The resort's in danger of going bankrupt."

"You should talk to Brooke. Forget that, I'll talk to Brooke."

"Down, boy."

Brooke is *not* like a sister to Kevin.

"Okay, admittedly that's weird," he said as he scratched his head again, "but not connected."

"I wouldn't think so. And then the feds asked me to look after a couple former mobsters who they think are here for some nefarious reason. And get this, one of them just happens to be Gia and Tony's grandpa."

He stopped in mid-chew, then finished slowly. Swallowed with a gulp. "Their grandpa's a Mafioso?"

"Former don of the Ravello Crime Family."

"What do the feds think is going down?"

"They have no idea."

"What do you think is going down?"

"I have no idea," I said, explaining what Brooke had heard about them "going to score this weekend" and how Gia practically bragged about running errands for Angelo years ago.

"So you think something with the sunglasses is connected to whatever they have going down this weekend?"

"Maybe. Or maybe somebody saw a chance to swipe a pair of Porsche shades worth three figures."

"Hmm. This burger's a little overdone."

"So go buy one at The Coconut."

"Hey, I'm only paid a *regular* salary."

"Yeah, yeah."

"So what are you going do to?" he asked after a couple bites.

"I didn't tell you the best part."

"This girl has a sister?"

"Angelo Ravello invited me to play poker with the gang tonight."

"He what?"

I explained how it had transpired at lunch while Kevin swigged from his bottle and moved on to burger number two. I had barely touched mine, so I finally paused and took a bite.

"This is great, man. This is your opening."

"Right. 'I raise you twenty, and by the way, if it doesn't mean you're going to shove me off the pier in cinderblock shoes, wanna clue me in to what you guys have cooking this weekend?'"

"Maybe don't word it that way."

"Kev, part of me thinks these guys might just be hanging out to relive the golden days. Wouldn't be the first time the feds got their shorts in a wad over nothing."

"Plus, you rat on Grandpa to the fibbies, it's gonna queer your deal with the babe."

I frowned at his terminology, then focused on eating. When we were done, he suggested we go get some ice cream, if there was time before poker. There was, but for several reasons I wasn't too keen on a Kevin-Brooke hookup, so I steered him away from it. Not in the mood for flying solo, he belched a few times and said he was heading home.

"You got plans for the weekend?" I asked.

"My cousin's buddy's taking me fishing tomorrow morning."

"Ocean fishing?"

"There another kind?"

"Good. Next time you can provide dinner."

"You mean once the girl heads back home?"

"Something like that."

"I'll be back mid-afternoon. Call if you need anything. You know, a sting to catch these candy thieves or something."

"I'll be sure to do that."

"Thanks for the burgers, Shades."

I nodded, he left, and I determined I had time to do dishes before hustling some old mobsters out of their ill-gotten wealth.

ELEVEN

I MORE OR LESS HATE DOING DISHES, BUT AT LEAST MY

sink is under a window so I can look out at palm trees and hedges dappled with the rays of the setting sun while I scrub. That works better when there aren't smudges on the window at eye level.

As I cleaned dried burger grease off a spatula, I replayed my conversation with Kevin through my head. It wasn't the first time I'd shared what was going on professionally with him. It helped me to process, even if all I got in return were smart-aleck comments and dumb ideas. But this time, maybe he'd hit on something.

"You buy your sister a really nice hat—"

"The kind that makes random dudes come up and hit on her?"

"Yeah. You buy her that hat, and then a cheapo pair of sunglasses?"

"Last thing I bought my sister was a pack of gum."

"I mean if you were a decent, caring human being."

"Maybe he's not. You said he was a weirdo."

"Then why the hat?"

There were really any number of reasons for buying her a nice hat and cheap sunglasses, say if the hat had been an actual thoughtful gift and the sunglasses a quick replacement because she'd lost hers. But I kept coming back to one thing.

"Maybe he's not. You said he was a weirdo."

It was a short sample, but Tony did strike me as a little self-obsessed, maybe a touch controlling.

"Maybe he's not."

I reached down to drain my water, wiped down the counter with a washcloth, then grabbed a towel to dry the dishes too. Picking up a plate, I looked out the window, right through a smudge.

Suddenly I remembered something else. I put the plate back in the rack, flopped the towel over it, and shook water off my hands as I walked across the kitchen to the refrigerator, where I had tossed Gia's sunglasses before talking to the feds. I pulled them out, glanced at them briefly, and then put them on.

As they had been beside the pool when I'd put them on briefly as a joke, they were smudged. I took them off, flipped on a light switch, and pulled out one of the chairs at my table. I sat down and examined them more closely. I reached into my pocket for a handkerchief and rubbed it over both sides of both lenses. I put them on again and looked at the light.

They weren't smudged, not with some snot-nosed kid's fingerprints or dirt, but something wasn't quite right. I took them off and set them on the table. They sat there while I dried the dishes and thought. It was eight-thirty, meaning I had time to change and walk over to the clubhouse, and a few minutes to spare. So I grabbed the glasses and took them to the small closet off the living room, next to the door to the deck. I rummaged around through an assorted mess of you-name-it until I found my small blacklight.

It was one of those hunches again, but I took the blacklight and the sunglasses into the bathroom and drew the shades. I put on the sunglasses, then clicked on the blacklight.

There were no smudges on the lenses.

There was, however, something on them. In five or six places on the lenses, very small, almost microscopic lines were drawn. I squinted, trying to make out what the lines were, but I couldn't focus at such a small scale and so close to one or the other eye. There was also what looked like text in a few places, and some of the lines had words or numbers beside them.

I tried adjusting the glasses on my nose a few times, to no avail. So I clicked off the blacklight and went back to the living room closet, where I rummaged around again and found a magnifying glass, a little slide-bar deal, not an old-fashioned Sherlock Holmes model. I returned to the darkness of the bathroom, clicked on the blacklight again, and this time held the sunglasses in my hand while holding the magnifying glass over them with the other.

The little lines were drawings of a part of a motor or an engine, then a section of what looked like housing or casing of some kind. The text areas, which I realized were small portions of assembly instructions, confirmed my suspicion. The drawings were specs for missile or rocket components, a missile or a rocket that made use of some sort of stealth technology.

I studied them for another minute, to see if I could determine any other details. Then I clicked off the blacklight and reached for the bathroom light switch. *"Maybe he's not,"* I muttered to myself.

Tony Ravello wasn't a sweet older brother who'd bought sunglasses for his sister when she'd lost hers. He had hidden or thrown away Gia's sunglasses, then "bought" her a replacement pair with the specs on them. She would wear them down to the pool, which had been his suggested activity while he went golfing, and would no doubt take them off to go swimming, giving the person Tony was passing the specs to an opportunity to lift them. A dead drop with an unsuspecting third party making the drop, rather a clever way of doing it really. He might even have given her the hat as a way to make her stand out, so the recipient would know which beautiful young lady's sunglasses to swipe.

It was a theory, of course, and raised a bunch of questions. Where had Tony gotten the specs in the first place, and who was he working for? They were in English, so were these specs to an American missile or rocket? Who was the buyer, and how was the payment transaction supposed to take place? Why had Tony inquired about Gia's sunglasses over cocktails? Confirming she'd made the pass? Or because the recipient had examined the sunglasses he'd swiped—mine instead of the real deal—and found no specs? Did Tony somehow suspect that I was the recipient, assuming he didn't know the recipient's face, because of the comments about Gia's hat and my presence with her? Were either of them, or I, in danger because the specs were now in my possession instead of the buyer's? And how did Angelo Ravello and his poker buddies tie into this, if at all? The fact that they were all retired mobsters couldn't be a coincidence, and yet I had never known the Mafia to be involved in selling state secrets.

I didn't have much time to think about it; I was due to meet said mobsters in the clubhouse in fifteen minutes. I returned the blacklight and magnifying glass to my living room closet, then took the sunglasses to the safe on the floor of my bedroom closet. Inside the safe is a false bottom with a separate combination. A little too James Bond, but in my line of work I sometimes have to keep things extra secure. I stashed the sunglasses there, returned the false bottom, and then set about changing.

I'd thrown on a T-shirt and shorts to grill burgers, and now put on a light blue Brookes Brothers dress shirt and a pair of white chinos. I rolled up the sleeves because I was suddenly a little warm and so a couple Goodfellas couldn't accuse me of hiding an ace up my sleeve. I was literally reaching for the doorknob when my doorbell rang.

It was Summer.

She still wore the same dress as that morning, now with a denim jacket. Her hair was loose, and I hated to admit that she was rather attractive. She looked like a girl on a college campus, not the manager of such a large resort. But I'd made the mistake of underestimating her abilities compared to her age one too many times already.

"Hi," I said. "What are you doing here?"

"I'm headed home for the night, but I wanted to check in with you beforehand."

"About?"

"May I come in?"

"Sure, but I've only got a minute."

"Hot date?"

"Poker."

She made a face of disapproval. I stepped back to let her in. Summer strode just far enough that I could close the door, then turned to look at me. "Have you done any investigating on the thefts from Sweet Creams?"

"I have."

"And?"

"And there isn't much to go on. We don't know when the thefts are happening, if it's a customer reaching around the counter or an employee loading up at the end of the night, if it's piece by piece or all at once. And, Summer, it is pretty minor on the scale of crimes."

"Wrong is still wrong."

"I know."

"Have you talked to any of the employees?"

"One."

"One? That's it?"

I sighed. "Look, I'll talk to some more tomorrow."

"What have you been doing all day, besides dating a client?"

"I would have informed you of my pursuits earlier had you not taken a half-day lunch."

Her usually jovial eyes now smoldered. She took a step closer. It suddenly smelled like oranges. "My personal life is none of your concern. Is that clear?"

"Crystal."

"You may have job security here because of my father's inexplicable fondness toward you, but you work for me, and I can do far worse things than fire you."

I exercised remarkable self-control and said nothing.

"Do your job, Gregg."

If I didn't know better, I'd have thought she pronounced the third G just to get at me. She gave me one last withering look, then turned. I pulled open the door just in time for her to storm through it, and I swung it shut behind her a little sharply. Then I took a few deep breaths, reminding myself not to blow the good thing I had going here.

In the morning, I would do everything I could to find the Sweet Creams candy thief, to keep Summer off my back.

That was, if I survived my night with the mob.

TWELVE

"I DON'T THINK YOU GOT 'EM." NICCOLO "NICKY"

Marino said, his dark eyes boring into me as he sucked in air, either keeping his dentures in place or trying to dislodge popcorn from his teeth.

I smiled on the inside but kept a stone face. Sucking his teeth was Marino's tell. After an hour of poker, I realized all the guys had one. Angelo "Angie" Ravello had an eyebrow twitch, which was noticeable given the squirrel's tail above his eye. Francesco "Frankie" Romano stacked and unstacked his chips, in correlation to the quality of his cards. And Vincenzo "Vinny" De Luca thought long and hard the better his hand. Amateur stuff, really. But no one ever said running criminal organizations made one good at card games.

"I call," Marino growled.

"Aces full of deuces," I said, setting my cards down on the felt.

Marino slammed down his cards and muttered something—likely curses—in Italian. I let a small smile escape my lips as I reached out and raked in another stack of chips. Like Kenny Rogers sings, you don't count your money while sitting at the table, but by my rough estimate, I was up over a grand. And this was penny-ante, just for fun stuff; I wasn't exactly making big money each hand.

And it was fun. I had entered the Gene E. Lowry Card Room on the backside of the clubhouse just after nine, full of jitters. It was fifty-fifty that Angelo and his cronies were part of Tony's tradecraft and fifty-fifty that, if so, I had been invited to this game in conjunction with that. One in four chance, then, I was walking into a hornets' nest. If so, they were incredibly coy.

The room features a standard poker table in the middle, with a couch and a pair of chairs on the perimeter. There is a fireplace, because it does occasionally get cool at night in Miami, and a bar the hotel keeps stocked for guests who reserve the card room. The usual assortment of interior flora and teak wainscotting on all four walls give the room a cozy feel, and the four mobsters made it hazy with their constant cigar smoke. There's only one window, looking out at the far western edge of the property, which is dreary in broad daylight because of all the palm trees but is just black at night.

In contrast to the dim environs, the four old guys had welcomed me as if I were Sal Manucci's boy from Staten Island with warm handshakes and slaps on the back. Almost before I could sit down, I had a cigar in one hand and a drink in the other, and they let me deal first. As I'd slowly taken their money in part due to pretty good cards and in part because they were so-so poker players at best, their warmth hadn't lessened, except maybe for Nicky Marino's.

"Get you another . . . what was it?" De Luca asked.

"Four horsemen," I said and handed him my rocks glass. "Thanks, Vinny."

Because I'd been brought up right, I had shown respect to my elders—mobsters or not—by referring to them as Mr. Ravello, Mr. De Luca, etcetera. They had quickly straightened me out and said it was Angie, Frankie, Nicky, and Vinny. Again, because my folks had trained me to, I didn't talk much, answering their questions about who I was and how long I'd been working as the "house dick" and if my intentions with Gia were pure. Before I could tell them they were, Vinny had asked who they were to question anybody on purity, and they'd all cackled until laughter became coughing.

That had been the theme of the night. The guys had drunk a lot of alcohol—and left to pee it out, in Nicky's case—and blown a lot of smoke, plus quite a bit of hot air. I had listened intently at first, thinking I could pick up something that would reveal their involvement with Tony and the spec-laden sunglasses or that might answer Costa and O'Connor's questions if the "score" they had cooking was unrelated. But they had given no hints, instead reliving the good old days, all without saying anything that could be construed as admission of specific criminal activities. They told stories of their youthful indiscretions, of hitting on broads at conventions, of a three-state car chase to catch a philandering girlfriend. Every hand was a new story that ended with them laughing and me getting richer. And, as the evening wore on, thinking less about gathering intel and more about enjoying their company.

Angie dealt the next hand, and for once I got junk. But because I was up, and just in case they had started to develop any sort of read on me, I decided to go for it anyhow.

"Kid, how long you say you've been at this gig?" Frankie asked. He hadn't changed from the afternoon, and I was grateful for the table blocking my view of his long, gnarly legs.

"About four years. One card," I said to Angie, even though I needed four. A good bluff has to be convincing.

"Two," Vinny said from my immediate left. "I guess you must have seen all sorts of characters come through here in that time."

Angie slid him two cards. "Dealer takes two," he said, then set the deck down.

"My fair share."

"Is it true what they say about this place?" Vinny asked.

"What's that?"

"You know, that it's kind of . . ." He looked to the other guys.

"A rendezvous for spies and hoods," Nicky said. "I'm in for five," he said, tossing a red chip onto a pile of white ones.

"Five," Frankie said beside me, and tossed in a chip.

I looked at my cards, even though I knew what I had. Three of clubs, three of hearts, six of diamonds, eight of spades, and jack of diamonds. I reached for my chips. "See your five, raise you five," I said, tossing in two red chips. Then I turned to Vinny. "It's true. We don't put it on the brochure, but it's true."

He looked at me, glanced at the pot, then put his cards face down. "Fold."

"Call," Angie said.

"Call," Nicky said.

Frankie took a red chip off his stack and set it on the felt. Then another. Then another. Two more. He shifted in his seat, which I'd gathered was not a tell but old age. Then he took one red chip and a blue and pushed them on the pile. "Raise you ten."

"Ten," I said, dropping one blue chip. "Why do you ask?" I said to Vinny, and then dropped two more blue chips. "Twenty more," I said to Frankie.

"You ever have dealings with any of them?"

"You mean, like playing poker with them?" I asked.

"Fold," Angie interjected.

"Naw, I mean . . . in official capacity."

"You mean have I ever had to bust a spy or a hood?"

"Or not bust one of them, you know, if it was one of our guys?"

I wasn't quite sure where he was going, but I got the sense he was fishing for something.

"By 'our' guys . . ."

"An American. Don't tell me we don't have spies and covert agents playing the game here too."

Nicky held up his cards, then laid them down. It was me and Frankie. He did nothing with his chips this time before raising me twenty more dollars. By my quick math, $150 sat in the pot, and I could either add $20 more of my own or fold. But I was having too much fun to fold.

"See your twenty," I said. I concluded Frankie's unstacking his red chips before had simply been determining which to use to raise, red or blue. I also concluded, by his lack of stacking or unstacking otherwise, he had neither a great hand nor a terrible hand. I could bluff him out of it. "And raise you . . . fifty," I said, pushing the necessary chips forward.

Nicky actually whistled. These guys had made a killing in the mob, but a few hundred bucks on a poker table was almost more than their tickers could take.

Frankie exhaled and mucked his cards. I would never know, but I was almost certain he could have beaten a pair of threes. I collected my chips again and began stacking them. "We do," I answered Vinny. "When you said 'our' guys, I thought you meant . . ." I lifted my chin and scratched my neck with the back of my hand.

Again I felt four sets of eyes on me, and again the tension was diffused when they broke into laughter. I took a swig of my drink, and, after asking permission, got another cigar from the humidor Angie had brought with them. Then, as the next hand played out, I told them the story of the time I had been *this* close to outing what I was sure was a Russian *femme fatale* who turned out to be a high-ranking member of the U.S. State Department facilitating back-office communication with the Israelis.

They in turn regaled me with more stories and continued to lose money. Having bankrupted Nicky earlier in the night, I finally cleaned out Frankie and Vinny with a king-high straight. It was quarter to midnight, and Angie, still having a few chips left, suggested we call it a night. I was up almost two thousand dollars and couldn't argue with him.

I got more handshakes and slaps on the back, and concluded these guys didn't really care about the money. Speaking of, it was a wad of cash kept in a drawer under the table, and Angie counted it out to me while the guys drained their glasses and puffed out their cigars. "We're playing again tomorrow night, if you want to join us again," he said, his telling eyebrow raised.

I looked at each of the guys, making sure they were okay with it. Nods confirmed it.

"Yeah, I'd love to."

"Bring that back with you," Vinny said, nodding at the stack of cash with an ear-to-ear grin.

"Every penny," I said.

"We're tapped on cigars," Frankie said, holding up an empty humidor. It was no wonder the way they'd been burning through them. "You think you could get your hands on some for tomorrow night?" he asked me with a wink.

Since I'd taken all their money, I figured it was the least I could do. "You got it, fellas."

We shook hands and slapped backs again, and I stuffed the cash in my pocket and headed back to my room, ready for some shut-eye after a long day. In almost three hours with the former dons, consiglieres, and underbosses, I hadn't picked up one iota of useful intelligence for Costa and O'Connor, or for myself. I'd gone in fifty-fifty that they were somehow working with Tony to pass secrets, and more or less convinced that, if not, they were up to something else criminal. I left thinking the feds had their intel wrong and had made me paranoid, and that all Angie and his pals had in mind was a fun weekend of reconnecting and remembering. And, based on their descriptions of several "young" women on the premises, maybe the "score" they had in mind was ending their night with someone other than me.

THIRTEEN

THE DAY'S ADVENTURES WERE NOT COMPLETE.

I walked across the mostly empty grounds and returned to my villa to find my gas fireplace crackling, sending flickering light across an otherwise dark living room and kitchen. Both rooms were empty. I closed the door quietly and slid my keys into my pants pocket that didn't have the poker winnings instead of hanging them on the hook. I stepped out of my Oxford leather slip-ons just in case whoever had lit the fire hadn't heard me come in. In so doing, I nearly tripped over a pair of women's sandals.

That eliminated Kevin and Lenny, the only two people who had keys to my villa—Kevin by my choice and Lenny because he could clone a keycard to any door on the property, for security purposes. In theory, Summer would have access to such a skeleton key, but she wouldn't use it unless it was an emergency. She also wouldn't have reason to light a fire unless I was tied to a stake in the midst of it.

I crept forward. I keep a Colt 1911 in my safe, which did me no good now if I had a prowler. But what kind of a prowler lights a fire in the fireplace?

I found out when I reached the top of the mini flight of stairs leading to the living room. At that moment, my bedroom door drew back, and Cari emerged. She wore a blue shirt with large white flowers on it, the tails tied above her midriff, and a short white skirt. She was barefoot, which explained the sandals, and her dark curly hair was now down, hanging around her shoulders. She held a glass of wine in her hand, which she had brought since I don't drink or keep wine. She took several steps forward and stopped, looking up at me demurely.

"Hello, Shades."

"Hello, Caridad."

I had used my clout as Head Security Officer to check into Cari in my spare time between cocktails and burgers with Kevin. Her full name was Caridad Álvarez, and she had checked into the hotel Thursday night for a long weekend. Room 512, for what that mattered. Per her hotel reservation, she was from Miami, age twenty-nine, and I was now reconsidering the theory that she was a working girl. Putting in late hours.

"What are you doing here?"

"I came to see you. You've been gone a while."

"Want to come in and wait until I get back?"

She grinned as if it was the funniest thing she'd ever heard. "I lit a fire," she said before taking a drink.

"How did you get in here?"

Caridad bit down on her lip. "I have my ways."

"Will I be needing to call a locksmith or a window repairman?" I asked, stepping down to her level.

"Let's not call anyone." She put the wineglass down on the coffee table, then put her hands on my arms and slid them under my rolled sleeves. "Not until morning at least."

The obvious physical appeal aside, I had no interest in Caridad or a one-night liaison with her, especially since I was dubious about her motivation. But I had to draw her out a little. So I took her shoulders, turned her, and pushed her down on the couch.

"Does Tony know you're here?" I asked, then turned to take my keys back to the hook by the door.

"Who?"

I hung them up and turned back around. "Handsome Italian guy, likes long walks on the beach, very clearly *not* part of the Mafia?"

Caridad ran her hand through her hair, leaning over the arm of the couch to look at me. "Tony made for a fun afternoon."

"And what, you saw me and realized I'd be a lot more fun?"

"Is that so hard to believe?"

"What took you so long?" I asked, coming back down the steps.

She frowned.

"Drinks were over at six. I was here until nine."

"I was waiting to make sure you did not have plans with Gia."

I nodded.

"I saw her by the pool, by herself, a little earlier, and figured you were available. I came here, found you gone, and waited."

"After breaking in."

Caridad stood. "Your deck door was open."

I pursed my lips. That was distinctly possible. I don't always remember to lock it at night. This is a rather secure property, after all.

She took hold of my arms again. "Is there something between you and her?"

"Not especially."

"Then I am sorry if I offended you by letting myself in."

"And starting a fire."

"And starting a fire," she said with a smile, her face now just inches from mine. "You're not angry about that, are you, Shades?"

"About the fire?"

"Or finding me waiting for you?"

"No, I'm not angry."

Caridad swung her hips and moved closer, her body now touching mine. "Then what do you say we have some fun? Let me pour you a glass of wine," she said, and started to step back. This time, I took her elbows and drew her close.

"There's just one problem with that," I said.

She blinked slowly and inched her head closer. "And what's that?"

"Your timing."

"My timing?"

"Yes. Well, technically mine I guess, because you were here earlier." I let go of her elbows and we separated a few inches. "I'm bushed."

"Bushed?"

"It's been a really long day, Cari, and . . . I need my sleep."

She stared at me for a moment. "You are serious?"

"I am. The American Journal of Medicine recommends adult males get no less than seven hours per night.

Caridad blinked slowly, then stepped back. She picked up her wineglass, stared at me for a moment, and then tipped it up and emptied it with a big swallow. She reached down and picked a purse off the coffee table, and, with one last look at me—a glare, really—she turned for the door. I followed her up the steps, and we stopped at the door.

"You could have just said no," she said. "You did not have to tease me."

"I wasn't teasing. Like I said, I'm exhausted and need my sleep."

She stepped into her sandals and looked at me one last time. "You can sleep when you are dead. But I could have made your dreams come true."

I stood at the door and watched her go, then closed—and locked—it behind her. I'd had plenty to drink for the day, but poured myself a small glass of cognac anyhow. I was exhausted, physically, but my mind was racing. I keep the cognac for just such situations.

Since there was a fire, I sat down on the couch and stared into it. For a few minutes, I thought about my reasons—other than not trusting Caridad—for not sleeping with her. I was tired, but not *that* tired. I sighed, swirled my cognac and took a sip, and moved on to the primary thing occupying my mind.

Tony Ravello was passing stealth missile technology to someone and using his sister as an unsuspecting mule—at least, I hoped she was unsuspecting. No, she had to have been, or she wouldn't have given me the glasses. Unless she thought I was the buyer and had made a preemptive move to approach her. Maybe "I like your hat" had sounded like a code to her. But if that was the case, why had she spent the day with me? Waiting for me to make payment? That seemed like a stretch, as there would be a protocol for that, and I doubted it involved lunch, tennis, and drinks on the roof. More likely she was being used by her brother and had liked my hair as much as I liked her hat.

Nothing Angelo Ravello and his pals had done during poker suggested they were involved in any way, nor could I figure out what that way might be. It was a coincidence, them inviting me to play, but coincidences—albeit rare—are part of life.

Speaking of coincidences, what was the deal with Caridad? Did she just glom onto random guys at the drop of a hat? Or had she been looking for something? It occurred to me that my villa was the second residence broken into without a trace that day. Could it have been Caridad who Gia and I had scared off after lunch? I remembered the woman on the security footage exiting a suite several down from Tony and Gia's. I hadn't seen her face, and her hair had been in a ponytail but . . . it could have been curly. It was hard to tell from grainy security camera footage. Had Caridad broken into Tony and Gia's suite looking for the specs, then come onto me when she hadn't found them there? Was that because she had scooped Gia's sunglasses by the pool and found nothing on them? Had someone else grabbed them before she could? Had the real buyer grabbed them, making Caridad a third party interested in the specs?

Then there was the petty theft from Sweet Creams and Diana Berglowe's fear of a jewel thief on the grounds—maybe one of those explained the break-in at Gia's—maybe it was another coincidence, the work of a random cat burglar. Could that explain Caridad's presence? She wasn't after the specs but after any expensive jewelry, say what might be found in Gia's suite or in my villa if she thought I had taken custody of Diana's pearls?

I watched firelight reflecting off my cognac before gulping the rest of it down. I laid my head back. A million questions and no answers, and now my mind was as exhausted as my body.

FOURTEEN

THERE IS NO WORSE INTERRUPTION IN LIFE THAN AN

alarm clock blaring one into consciousness from a sound sleep. Which is why, unless a drastic situation calls for it, I never set one. I'm also pretty good at waking within fifteen minutes—half hour max—of the time I intend to the night before. Thus I was both bewildered and annoyed when my alarm went off Saturday morning, rousing me at . . . 8:36 a.m.?

My bewilderment grew. I was pretty sure I hadn't set it in the first place, and I certainly hadn't set it for such a weird time.

Another wave of consciousness washed over me, and I realized the noise was more of a chirp and less of a ring, and that there were interludes of silence between the chirps. It wasn't my alarm clock, but my phone.

I rolled over, swiped for my nightstand, and came up with a handful of receiver. "Shades," I mumbled.

"Pull up the shades and drag yourself out of bed."

"Good morning to you too, Summer."

"Your services are needed in Room 404," she said.

"Why," I asked as I rubbed my hand over my face, "what's going on?"

"A guest has been murdered."

Fully awake, I ran through the shower, threw on some clothes, and hurried over to the main building. It was another warm, sort of hazy morning, and the air-conditioned interior of the hotel was a respite after just a few minutes outside. Since it was a Saturday, and fairly early, the grounds and atrium were mostly empty. I took the elevator to the fourth floor, where Summer was waiting in the hallway with Lenny and a short maid who was rambling in incoherent Spanish.

"What happened?" I asked.

"Lenny, would you go wait for the police?"

"Yes, Miss Dawson."

She turned to me. "Mr. Stewart was due to check out this morning, so Consuela went to clean the room. She found him like that," Summer said, nodding at the ajar door to Room 404. It faced north, toward the pool area, but as I entered ahead of her, I saw the drapes in the living room were drawn. The only light came from directly over the entry, the main light activated by the switch by the door. It was enough to reveal a mess in the living room. Couch pillows on the floor, a plant tipped over and dirt on the carpet, and two of four legs on the coffee table broken, the glass surface cracked and shattered.

On the wall by the door to the bedroom, a splotch of brown was likely dried blood, just above a pair of men's(?) Birkenstocks, one of which faced the wall, one of which was cockeyed and half on top of the other. The table and chairs in the kitchenette were askew, and there was more blood on the bedroom door jamb. There was no body, and, sensing my knowledge of that, Summer said from behind me, "In there."

I took a step toward the bedroom, but stopped when an object on the living room floor caught my eye. A pair of sunglasses. Porsche Design by Carrera aviator sunglasses with orange and purple lenses, to be exact. My sunglasses, that I had given Gia and that been stolen from her while she swam. I wondered if Lenny or Summer had seen them and concluded they were mine, but decided not to bring it up. Instead, I nudged open the mostly closed bedroom door and stopped again.

The lamp in the corner, controlled by the light switch by the door, was on, lightening an otherwise dark room, thanks to drawn shades and blinds. A chair by the dressing table was tipped over, and the most of the bedding was torn off the bed and piled on the floor at its foot. Lying on top of the bedding, a sheet around the neck like an aviator's scarf, was the dead man's body.

He was white—or had been, now a pale greenish-gray color—with dark closely cut hair. He wore a polo shirt and shorts, no socks or shoes, no jewelry. I wasn't squeamish, but the dead guy's wide-open eyes staring at the ceiling weren't something I needed before breakfast.

I turned back to Summer. "Anybody touch anything?"

"Consuela flipped on the lights and opened the door. Also closed it behind her, apparently. That's it."

"Who is he? You said his name was Stewart?"

"Martin Stewart, from here in Miami. Checked in Thursday night."

I turned back to the body. "He looks familiar."

"He's a repeat guest. Four, maybe five times per year."

"Traveling alone?"

"According to his reservation, yes."

I took a few steps forward.

"I think we should probably let the cops handle this."

"You called me."

"I wanted you to be aware of what happened on your watch. I didn't mean for you to investigate the crime."

"It is my job, and my watch," I said. I turned back and scanned the bedroom, then walked into the attached bathroom. A garment bag hung on a rack on the back of the door. I used a knuckle to draw the flap open, enough that I could see a couple shirts and a pair of slacks. A men's toiletry kit sat on the double vanity. There was nothing else of interest.

"What are you looking for?"

"Signs that he had a companion, a roommate, a guest."

"See any?"

"No. And he traveled light."

"Did you see the sunglasses in the living room?" she asked. "They look kind of like yours."

I analyzed Summer's face. I didn't think she was implying anything. So I grinned. "Guess he had good taste."

The cops arrived two minutes later, scolded us briefly for entering the room a second time, and then began stringing up crime scene tape and conducting their investigation. Summer gave Consuela the rest of the day off and hurried off to start damage control, what with having a murdered guest being bad PR for a hotel. That left Lenny and I in the hallway to answer the cops' questions, and me to answer Lenny's. He was thinking out loud, and I mumbled canned responses while doing some of my own thinking.

Sure, it was possible Martin Stewart just happened to have owned a pair of sunglasses like the ones I had given Gia and someone had stolen from her, and it was possible a man who hadn't so much as left out a coffee mug had tossed them on the coffee table after going for a walk on the beach. But the weekend had already used up its allotment of coincidences. That left me three reasonable conclusions:

Martin Stewart was the buyer, and he had swiped Gia's sunglasses, thinking they contained the missile specs.

Stewart was a thief who had swiped the sunglasses, either because they fetched $150 on the street or because he knew of the deal and suspected they contained the missile specs.

Or Stewart was a broker and had swiped the sunglasses to pass to a third-party buyer.

In the first case, he could have been killed by a third party, by the seller (say, if payment wasn't received), or by the "good guys" who wanted to keep the specs from falling into the wrong hands.

In the second case, he could have been killed by the same group of people or by the actual buyer whose deal he had screwed up.

In the third case, he would most likely have been killed by a third party.

Whatever the case, the only reason I could think for the sunglasses still being there was that the killer had examined them and found out they weren't the right pair, that they didn't contain the specs. That would put the seller in danger, or whoever the killer thought had the real glasses.

Or the sister/weekend date of said person.

One thing I knew, finding a candy thief had plummeted on the list of the day's priorities.

FIFTEEN

Tony and Gia found me in the atrium, not far from

the stacking slider doors that open more than a dozen feet wide to let the tropical breeze in. He wore a white shirt, open a few buttons, sunglasses hanging over the highest button, and khaki shorts. Gia wore a white and green chevron patterned dress and slides, her hair sadly in a ponytail.

"We heard a guest was murdered," Tony said, dropping his chin and his tone.

I nodded, since there was no use denying it. Watching both of their faces, but his more, I said, "A man named Martin Stewart."

"Who was he?" Gia asked.

"Just a guest," I lied with a shrug.

"Who kills just a guest?"

"That's what the cops are trying to figure out."

"The cops. Not the hotel detective?" she asked, sincerely but with a little teasing in her eyes.

"Murder's a little over my paygrade."

"But they're keeping you in the loop, surely," Tony said. "They have to, right; this is your hotel, your responsibility."

"They're keeping me apprised."

"Any leads?"

I nodded toward the doors, preferring to take this conversation away from people. Truth is, I never would have had the conversation with guests if I didn't seriously believe one or both of them was potentially responsible and/or in danger. But I figured I had to give to get.

We exited onto a wide sidewalk, flanked by hedges and uniform cherry palms that led to the giant oak tree. "Nothing so far," I said in response to Tony as we walked. "They figure he was killed yesterday morning, judging by the state of the body. The M.E. will have an exact time after the autopsy."

"How was he killed?"

"Strangled," I said. "Looked like quite a fight beforehand." I positioned myself to see both of their faces again. "Whoever killed them took a shot to the back of the head." This I knew because the cops had searched Stewart and found a scrape on his arm that could have accounted for the blood on the door jamb, but no wound on his head. That meant the splotch of blood on the wall belonged to whoever killed him.

"No motive?" Tony asked. "No stash of cash or anything found in his room?"

"A stash of cash?" Gia asked.

He shrugged. "Like if some deal was going down or something. Why else would a random guy be killed?"

"And you think the killer killed him for a stash of cash and then left it?"

He shrugged again. "I don't know."

"There was nothing," I said.

"So . . ." Gia said, looking down, "the killer is still at large? Is it safe here?"

I remembered the break-in to her room the day before, a break-in that had happened several hours after Stewart had been killed. I remembered my theory that Tony had been passing missile specs via sunglasses, that Stewart had died in possession of sunglasses he most likely believed to contain those specs but that did not. But I wasn't quite ready to share theories with Tony and Gia.

"Unless you have a reason to think the same person would be after you."

"Who would be after us?" Tony said, and said it convincingly. "I mean, it's not like we have any valuables hidden under the bed." He nudged his sister's arm. "Wanna grab some breakfast?"

"I'm not very hungry," she said.

"Suit yourself. Shades, I'll see you later."

"Tony," I said and shook his hand. Then he was off.

I turned to Gia. "If no breakfast, how about a cup of coffee?"

"Okay," she said with a smile.

I thought about taking her back to my villa, but the way this was going, Diana Berglowe would be there in a nightgown. So we went to the Circle Bar, which serves more than just alcohol. We ordered two cups of coffee and sat by ourselves at the end of the bar. It was quarter after ten, and the pool deck was just coming to life. Even so, we had privacy.

"Can I ask you something?" I said.

"Um-hmm."

"When Tony asked you about your sunglasses yesterday, on the roof, why didn't you tell him the truth?"

She eyed me over her mug, which she blew into. "What, you mean that they were so ugly I traded them to you?"

I shrugged. "If they were just a last-second replacement purchase, would it have really hurt his feelings?"

"Probably not. But I felt a little bad about it and, besides, they were stolen anyhow." She finally took a sip from her mug.

So did I, mulling. That was plausible. And I couldn't think of a reason for her to lie to me now, a way that she was involved in this other than innocently. Not one that made sense with all I knew.

"Why do you ask?"

"Just curious."

She nodded. "My turn?"

I nodded in return.

"Who is Martin Stewart really?"

"You don't believe me?"

"I believe what you told us, more or less. But there's got to be more to it than that."

"I agree. But I don't know what it is."

"You think the person who killed him is the same person who broke into our suite?"

And possibly my villa last night?

"I think it's possible."

"Why?"

"I don't know."

She took another sip, looking at me over the rim of her mug. "Now I don't believe you."

I sighed. "Gia, is there any chance at all your grandfather and his pals are here to do more than play poker and shuffleboard and talk about the good old days?"

"Like what?"

"Nobody really retires, not for good, from the Family."

"Maybe, maybe not." Gia set her mug down. "I've never pretended Grandpa Angie was the most wholesome person on the planet, but he's never looked me in the eye and lied to me either. When he suggested this trip, I asked why, and he said 'Because I'm getting old and want to have a good time while I still can.' I took him at his word."

"So the trip was his idea?"

She nodded.

"And he invited you and Tony?"

"Yep."

"How long ago?"

She closed one eye. "Why? What are you getting at?"

"Just humor me."

"Fourth of July weekend."

Far enough out for Tony to plan a drop. Plenty of time. I took a drink and set my mug down as well.

Gia eyed me for a second, then leaned forward. She placed a hand on my knee. "Shades, will you tell me the truth?"

I looked into her brown almond eyes and nodded. "I will."

"Am I in danger?"

I scrunched up my face for just a second. "I can't say for sure you're not. I don't have any reason to think you are, specifically, but you might want to stick close to someone you trust."

"Like you?"

"I would, but I have a few errands to run this morning."

"Still the truth?"

"I wouldn't pass up spending time with you if I didn't have to."

"I guess I could read by the pool. Nothing will happen to me there."

"Not if you keep your sunglasses on your head."

Gia smiled. "And Grandpa Angie and the guys want me to play shuffleboard with them after lunch. Truth is," she said, leaning in a little more, "I think they just like to be around our generation to feel young."

Her saying that made me wonder again why they had wanted to play poker with me. I let it go for the time being as we finished our coffee and split up. I had told her the truth, I did have errands to run. First up, convincing Summer to let me have a second look at Martin Stewart's room.

SIXTEEN

Miami detectives, according to my limited ex-

perience with them and from what I've heard from reliable sources, are about ten-percent corrupt, ten-percent under the thumb of the cocaine dealers, and eighty-percent dang good cops. The two who had responded to Stewart's death struck me as being in the latter group, but being a dang good cop did not make one perfect. And something Tony had said and something Summer had said and something I remembered had all coalesced in my mind while having coffee with Gia.

Summer was not in her office. Her secretary, Helaine, was. Helaine is a sweet old woman who can't hear a lick and who moves about as fast as the torpid backwaters of the Everglades. But she keeps Tootsie Rolls on her desk, and not for her because they would pull out her dentures. (Her statement, not my assumption.) Helaine is the gatekeeper to Summer's office, as well as that of the Assistant

Manager and Chief of Hospitality, and—sweet or not—she takes her duty seriously. She's as loyal to Summer as the day is long, and guards Summer's privacy almost as much as Summer does. I learned the only way to get on Helaine's bad side, other than to hurry her along in a story about one of her grandchildren, is to disrespect Summer or her time or her privacy. So I always go through the song-and-dance with Helaine, and thus factor an extra five to ten minutes into every visit.

On this occasion, with the murder of Stewart still recent, Helaine was somber and thus we breezed through the formalities. I was also able to cite the murder of Stewart as reason for her to dig up some information for me. Not without a five-minute dissertation from her about why the cops weren't handling this. But eventually, she confirmed my hunch—Martin Stewart always stayed in Room 404 when he visited The Grandeur Hotel & Resort.

Summer did not return during our conversation, nor did Helaine know where she was. Or so she said. More likely she knew and wasn't telling. Whatever the case, I assumed Summer's permission and headed up to the 4th floor. Police tape still crisscrossed the door, which meant Miami P.D. wasn't through with their investigation. I used a skeleton key Lenny most certainly *did not* give me to let myself into the room.

Having watched way too many cop shows where somebody broke into a room, didn't lock the door behind them, and then got whacked over the head from behind, I deadbolted the door. Too bad Martin Stewart hadn't been so clever. Or had he admitted his killer? Or had he—or she—snuck in from the balcony? The cops would have checked all that, and would report to Summer, who would dutifully tell me. I didn't question their competence, but maybe their hunches.

Stewart's body was gone, and so was his garment bag, his toiletry kit, the Birkenstocks from outside the bedroom, and the sunglasses—my sunglasses—from on top of the broken glass of the coffee table. All had been "tagged and bagged," I was sure. The small in-room safe, tucked in the bottom drawer of the nightstand, was open. Either Stewart hadn't used it, or the cops had found whatever was there. I guessed the former and set about looking for telltale signs. There were none, so I resorted to old-fashioned hard work.

I'd read a story a few years back in the *Herald* about a broker for one of the cartels, a guy who made a living passing coke to buyers and dough to sellers. He frequented half a dozen hotels, used them to make deals, and they figured over the course of several years before the cops busted him, tens of thousands of dollars and dozens of kilos of cocaine had passed through some of these hotels. It had not, however, been stored in the in-room safes. Rather, the broker had brought his own safe, hidden it in the room (in this case in one of the air vents), and always returned to the same room where he utilized his very own safe.

If my third possible case was true, and Stewart had been a broker, then maybe he'd been responsible for swiping the sunglasses, verifying their legitimacy, and then getting them to the buyer and the buyer's money to the seller. In such an instance, he would need a place to keep the money safe. But to find it.

I checked all the air vents and found nothing but lint. I checked the toilet tank and found nothing but water. I checked behind and inside furniture, looked for a loose baseboard or carpet that might have recently been pulled up, and was about to check the sink and shower drains when I decided to sit down to think. I was in the bedroom, on the end chair, looking across the bed and through the door to the front door. I found myself replaying events.

Stewart had been on the couch, with the sunglasses out, maybe to examine them, although there hadn't been a blacklight found on his person or in the room. The killer had entered, the how still being a mystery, and they had engaged in a struggle that had collapsed the coffee table and kicked over the plant. Stewart had gotten the better of it, slamming the killer into the wall above his sandals, cracking their head on the wall or smearing blood from earlier in the fight on it. The killer had then spun him around, into the kitchen table and chairs, before the two of them spilled into the bedroom. They had fallen on the bed, fighting and clawing, until the killer had managed to wrap the sheet around Stewart's neck and choke him out. I closed my eyes, trying to picture Caridad's arms. Did she have the physique to do it? Problem was, when I closed my eyes and pictured Caridad, her arms didn't jump to the forefront.

Kicked over the plant . . .

I stood and walked back to the living room. The plant was right where it had been, tipped over beside the loveseat on the wall against the bedroom. Dirt had tumbled out onto the carpet, but much of it remained in the pot. After a moment's hesitation, I finished the job, emptying it all onto the carpet.

I sighed. No safe hidden in the bottom of the pot.

I stood, and as I did, something metallic caught my eye. I squatted down and brushed aside some dirt to reveal a small key on a ring.

I stood again, swinging the key on the ring. I looked around, and my eyes rested on another potted plant beside the TV. If I was wrong, Summer would kill me. But I wasn't wrong. I tipped over the plant and a safe the size of a Bible or a small textbook tumbled out along with the dirt. I brushed and blew it off, then took the safe over to the table and sat down.

The key fit, and I lifted open the lid on the small strongbox. There was no cash. But there was another key, also on a ring, with a number stamped on the side, as well as a journal or notebook bound with a rubber band, and a flashlight. Correction, a blacklight, I discovered as I clicked it on and off.

So had Stewart been interrupted before he could rummage through the dirt for his key and strongbox to get his blacklight to inspect the sunglasses, or had he already done so and found them to be the wrong pair? No way to know, so I examined the other contents again.

The key was a locker key, say from the airport or a bus or train station, or a roller-skating rink or bowling alley for that matter. I pocketed it. Then I unsnapped the rubber band from the book. It didn't take long for me to discover that it was a ledger—names or initials or code words next to more code words next to numbers next to checkmarks. The names of people who owed him, what they owed him for, the amount they owed, and whether or not they had paid. I flipped to the end of the notes and found three entries with no checkmark.

Boots – Piggies – 5

Cincy – Minnie – 250

Arnold – Lucy – ▱

None of it made sense. Niccolo Marino was from Cincinnati, so was the word "Cincy" a reference to him? Could "Lucy" be short for LSD? Was "Lucy" the name and "Arnold" the clue? Same with

"Cincy" and "Minnie"? Was it a Disney reference, to Minnie Mouse? And why the drawing of a flag instead of a dollar figure for the last one?

I flipped through a few pages of the ledger, trying to figure out the pattern used, but it was too vague. The only thing I concluded was somebody owed Stewart 5, 250, and a flag, and I was willing to bet a few zeros or the letter K was missing after the numbers. That, and something in that ledger told me who killed him and why.

SEVENTEEN

After being briefed by the Miami detectives and

before going downstairs and meeting Tony and Gia, I had used Summer's phone—with permission, of course—to make a call. It had been a bit of a flyer, given the previous night, but after an apology, I had convinced Caridad to have lunch with me at noon. She'd opted for the rooftop bar, which opens at eleven on weekends. So I left Stewart's room with the key and ledger in my possession, figuring I'd notify the cops at some point, and hurried back to my villa to clean up. I put on a plaid shirt with black collar and cuffs, left one extra button open, and added a splash of Dior Eau Sauvage, and headed out.

I made it only to the large oak tree. Diana Berglowe was sitting on one of the benches under the tree. "Mr. Shades," she called, turning my attention.

"Miss Berglowe," I said. We were in the shade, so I removed my sunglasses. Diana wore a long, flowing brown dress—a caftan, I think they call it—with an Eastern print on it. She was well accessorized again, and her hair was in the same low ponytail as the day before.

"Thank heavens, I have been looking for you most of the morning. I just sat down to rest a moment."

"I'm sorry," I said, approaching her bench. "May I?"

"Please."

"Is something the matter?"

"I heard there's been a murder on the grounds."

"Word travels fast."

"Was anything of value taken?"

"It doesn't appear so."

"May I ask, Mr. Shades, what the motive was?"

"I'm afraid we don't know," I said, remembering the ledger and key that were now back in *my* safe, along with the cheapie sunglasses containing missile specs. Quite a collection I was amassing. "The police haven't uncovered anything."

She wrung her hands.

I placed mine on top of hers. "What's wrong, Diana?"

She lifted those marvelous blue eyes to meet mine. "I've changed my mind, and wonder if you might not hold onto my pearls for me?"

"I certainly can, if it would make you feel better, but there's also the safe in your suite, or the hotel safe."

"I'd feel so much better if you would hold onto them, with everything that's going on. The murder, and I saw a man lurking in the lobby last evening. I'm certain he was watching me."

"What did he look like?"

"He was tall, dark hair, swarthy. He might have been an Arab. Dressed very casually. And . . ." Her expression turned bashful. "He was wearing sunglasses inside."

"Did he make any sort of threatening move? Did he follow you? Have you seen him again since?"

She shook her head to all questions. "I'd just feel so much better if you would hold onto them."

"Of course. I'm afraid I'm late for an appointment right now, but I can arrange to pick them up after lunch."

"How about I meet you right back here? Say one-fifteen? If anyone is watching me or my room, your coming there would certainly tip them off."

Diana's paranoia was getting the best of her, but I didn't want to be rude. Besides, a cloak-and-dagger exchange under the oak tree sounded like fun. "That will be fine. One-fifteen."

"I'll meet you right here, with the pearls," she said.

I patted her hand and stood to leave.

"Thank you, Mr. Shades."

"You're quite welcome."

I waited to frown until I'd turned away from her. I was still pretty sure Diana had nothing to fear, swarthy potential Arabs looking at her or not. And I didn't think there was any real danger in her bringing me the pearls, not in public in broad daylight. But, the nagging voice in my head reminded me someone had broken into Gia's suite and someone had killed Martin Stewart. Those seemed to be disconnected from Diana's pearls, but I couldn't entirely rule out the existence of a cat burglar on the premises. To that end, I hoped my lunch with Caridad would help me determine whether or not—or, more accurately, how exactly—she was involved in all this.

EIGHTEEN

CARIDAD WAS WAITING AT ONE OF THE TABLES BY THE

railing at the rooftop bar, a mimosa in front of her half gone. She wore a yellow shirtdress with a black belt. Her hair was piled on top of her head again, held with a band to match the dress. There was just enough room for a pair of Ray-Ban wayfarer sunglasses to be perched in front of the updo.

"Thanks for meeting me, Cari," I said as I pulled out a chair across from her.

"You said you wanted to apologize."

"And I do."

She shook her head. "There's no need. Believe it or not, Shades, you're not the first person to turn down my advances."

"I'm not sure I do believe that," I said, "but that's not what I wanted to apologize for."

Caridad took a slow pull on her mimosa. "Then what?"

"I was a little bit of a tease last night. What can I say, you caught me off guard and, well . . ." I flashed my most disarming smile, pure gold, "I prefer to be the one to make the advances."

"A self-proclaimed chauvinist."

"Old-fashioned, maybe."

"Are you here now to make advances?"

"Let's start with lunch."

Her smile, for the first time, seemed genuine. I went to the bar and placed our order, then rejoined her.

"So what brings you to The Grandeur?"

"Stress," she said straightaway. "Work is a grind, and if I try to relax at home, it invariably sucks me back in."

"How long have you been with your current firm?"

"Since law school."

"That can't have been long," I said.

"Three years."

"Where'd you go?"

"The U."

"Hmm."

"What's 'Hmm'?"

"Oh, nothing."

She probed into my background a little, and I gave her the truth in so far as it didn't compromise the real reason for this luncheon. We went back and forth until chicken and cheese quesadillas with chips and salsa arrived. I learned nothing from the point-counterpoint, especially since I didn't know if she was telling the truth.

"Did you hear about the murder?" I asked while loading a chip with salsa.

"What murder?" she asked with appropriate surprise on her face. She paused but then picked up a quesadilla wedge.

"One of the guests in the hotel." I watched her while I ate the chip. Then I licked my lips. "A man named Martin Stewart, strangled by his bedsheet."

"How gruesome. Do you have any suspects? Or is this a police matter?"

"No and yes."

She nodded. "When did it happen?"

"Sometime mid- to late-morning yesterday."

"Is that why you were a little standoffish last night?" she asked. "Your own work stress?"

"His body wasn't found until this morning."

Caridad took a bite, chewed, swallowed. She flitted her eyebrows up. "Is that the real reason for lunch, to eliminate me as a suspect?"

She said it teasingly, and it worked to disarm me. I said no, because the alternative was to cease efforts to be coy. Not that they were getting anywhere.

"I told you, the police are handling it."

"Why not the hotel detective?" she said, holding up a chip as if it were a strawberry dipped in chocolate before sticking it in her mouth.

"He's otherwise engaged," I said.

"Smooth. Well, for the record, I have no alibi whatsoever."

I raised an eyebrow.

"I got in late Thursday night, slept in, ordered room service, and read some briefs on the balcony."

"Read some briefs?"

"My firm wouldn't let me take a *whole* extended weekend off."

I nodded, wondering why she was volunteering her lack of alibi. I sensed it was similar to why some animals played with their prey before eating it. But I still wasn't sure I was getting an accurate read on her.

"They did bring me some eggs, toast, and orange juice around ten o'clock."

"I'll be sure to tell the cops that if they ask."

"Besides, why would I want to kill Martin Stewart?"

"Why would anyone?"

She shrugged and lifted another quesadilla wedge.

I ate my own wedge, pondering this woman who had come up to Tony—a decent enough looking guy, I suppose, and I hadn't even seen him in his bathing trunks—and then tried to seduce me that night, and now was teasing me about Stewart's murder.

"You know," she said, leaning forward. There was nobody around us, so she had no reason to fear being overheard. "If I were you, I would check out Tony's grandfather."

"Why is that?"

"Isn't it obvious? Tony admitted he was in the Mafia."

"Had been in the Mafia, but that might be a distinction without a difference."

"The Mafia's always killing people. There wasn't a bloody horse's head in the bed, was there?"

"No. Blood on the wall, which we think was the killer's," I said, watching her face.

It gave away nothing. She ate a chip. "Well, that's where my money is."

"Why?"

"I just told you why."

"No, I mean why would the Mafia kill Stewart? I mean, sure, they're always bumping people off, but they have a reason."

"What do you know about him?"

"Not much. Cops might know more. He's a repeat customer."

"Maybe he does business with them often. Maybe he's some kind of broker or something."

That made two of us with that theory.

We finished our lunch, and both said, "I have a question," at the same time.

"Ladies first," I said.

She raised her chin a fraction. "Who was the lady you were with?"

"Last night? Gia Rav—"

"No, under the oak tree, just before you came up here. I saw you through the branches. I saw you hold her hand."

There wasn't a trace of jealousy in her tone, nor on her face. And the lack of it kept me from telling her the whole truth.

"A guest, concerned about the recent goings on at the hotel. I placed a hand on hers to comfort her."

She seemed to buy it. Then frowned. "Goings on—plural?"

"Leads to my question. Which room are you in?"

"Two-sixteen."

"And where were you yesterday afternoon around one-fifteen, one-thirty?"

Caridad briefly looked down and to the side. She raised her head. "On my way to the beach. Why?"

"There was a break-in at a guest's room, and they escaped via the balcony. But we have no witnesses. I'm looking for anybody who might have seen anything."

She shook her head. "Not a thing."

I nodded.

"I suppose you have all sorts of important things to do this afternoon," she said.

"I do indeed."

"Hmm. Then I'll have to go for a walk on the beach by myself."

"Not for long, I imagine."

Her evil eye broke into a smirk. "Well, you know which room I'm in," she said. "And I'm sure someone with your job can get a keycard to any room in the hotel."

"Want me to come over and light a fire and drink some wine while you're gone?"

Still smirking, she stood and traced my arm with her finger. "Thanks for lunch, Shades." Then she flipped down her Ray-Bans and strutted toward the elevator.

NINETEEN

I SPENT A FEW MORE MINUTES AT THE TABLE, SINCE I HAD

time before meeting Diana again to collect her pearls. I thought through everything Caridad had said—and what she *hadn't* said— and how she'd said or not said it. I was pretty sure we'd just played a game of cat-and-mouse, but I wasn't sure who was the mouse and who was the cat.

I was also pretty sure Caridad hadn't spent the entire previous morning in her hotel room. But the fact that she told me she had, instead of saying "I lounged around the pool; surely someone saw me" suggested that maybe she wanted an alibi from being around the pool too. That put her back square in my crosshairs for being the specs buyer and thus the killer. But if she had nabbed Gia's sunglasses while she swam, how had they ended up in Stewart's room? Was she a broker, a middle-woman, who had delivered them to him, then killed him for some reason? Delivered them and *not* been the one to kill him?

I had a few minutes yet before meeting with Diana, but that wasn't enough time to check in with Summer to see if she'd heard from the cops working the case. I needed to tell them about the ledger and the key, but I kind of wanted to take my crack at them first. Not that I didn't trust the detectives, like I said. But it would be hard to explain all the context of random events going on at the resort over the weekend, and I was sure some of them tied in to Stewart's murder somehow. Besides, it wasn't like the detectives hadn't had their chance to search the room, and that tipped over plant had basically been begging to be searched for a key.

So I opted for a stroll through the pool deck. That meant taking the elevator down to the east end of the hotel. I exited to the shuffleboard courts, which were empty, meaning Gia and her grandpa were still at lunch. I passed by a small patio seating area around a firepit and came out through a strand of palms to the pool deck. Maybe half the chairs and chaise lounges around the two pools were occupied, and a dozen people filled each pool. Across the way, a third of the stools and tables at the Circle Bar were occupied. Flesh tone—everything from pasty white to tanned to sunburned red to brown to black—was the dominant color, with the full spectrum of the rainbow speckled in. That made the two stiffs in camp shirts stand out. One of them wore shorts revealing very white legs and feet; the other slacks and slide sandals. If you've never seen a pair of FBI agents in casual beachwear, count your blessings.

"Mr. Pulaski," Agent Costa hailed from a rattan seating area backed by a hedgerow between the pools. He wore the shorts, and was sitting, and there was way more leg than a guy needed to see this soon after a meal. Or anytime. Agent O'Connor stood beside him in the slacks, trying to look casual and failing miserably.

"Gentlemen," I said, stopping in front of them.

"Do you have a few minutes?" O'Connor asked.

I checked my watch, purely to make a point. I knew what time it was. "A few," I said.

"Have a seat," Costa said, gesturing at the chair beside him. I took one on the other end of the seating area, away from the legs. I was still close enough to converse.

O'Connor sat too, on the same couch as Costa, who then said, "We're wondering if you've made any progress in your investigation."

"You're okay discussing that out here, in the open?"

"There's silence in all the shouting," O'Connor said. I wasn't sure if that was profound or stupid, but a girlish scream and an immediate splash from the pool to the left drove home his point. So did Phil Collins on the pool deck speaker system.

"I haven't gathered much," I said, leaning in slightly.

"Have you made contact with them?" Costa asked. "With the granddaughter?"

"I have."

"And?"

"She is cute."

O'Connor rolled his eyes.

"She thinks she's here because her grandpa sprang for a vacation to spend valuable time with his grandkids while he still can."

Costa perked up. "Is there a health scare?"

"Try not to get so excited," I said. "No. He's just an old man and old men eventually die."

"Have you learned anything?" O'Connor asked.

I hadn't seen the two fibbies around the grounds, and they were hard to miss. So I concluded they had spent most of their time in their room with a glass against the wall and thus wouldn't know I was holding back.

"No. I've spent some time with the granddaughter, probed a little, but I don't think she knows anything. I actually don't think there's anything to know. And I did meet the guys."

"You met them?" Costa asked.

"Kinda buried that, didn't you?" O'Connor said.

I held out my hands. "You asked multiple questions, and I picked the one to answer first. Yes, they ran into us while we were having lunch, I was introduced . . ."

"What is it?"

I wasn't sure, but something about our interaction suddenly bugged me. Or rather, bugged my subconscious, that little pest.

"Nothing," I said. "They seemed to like me and invited me to play poker with them. Said they needed a fifth."

"Poker?" Costa nearly bounced out of his seat. "When? Where?"

"Tonight," I said, figuring there was no point bringing up last night's game. "And I'm not telling you where because I don't need three parabolic mics and a camcorder pointed at the windows. Look, you asked me to do a job and I'm doing it. I'll chat them up, have a few drinks, and if there's anything going down, I'll get the sense of it. But if you guys get all antsy and start snooping in the bushes, they'll go quiet, and I'll probably end up as shark food."

"All right," Costa said, holding up his hand. "All right. We'll stand down. But you keep us in the loop."

"I will."

"Tonight, you said?"

"Yes."

They looked at each other. "I just hope it doesn't go down before then," O'Connor said.

I looked at my watch again, even though I knew I still had time. "Now, if you gentlemen will excuse me, I do have another appointment."

"Of course, Mr. Pulaski," Costa said. "Thanks for your time."

I nodded and stood to leave.

"Oh, Mr. Pulaski," O'Connor said. "We hear you caught a murder investigation."

I stepped closer. "I didn't catch anything. The cops are handling it."

"You'll let us know if the victim has any underworld connections, won't you?"

"You don't liaise with the cops?"

"We're trying to keep a low profile."

I raised an eyebrow at their attire.

"I tell you what."

They leaned forward.

"Stop by Miss Dawson's office. She'll give you the detectives' names, and you can ask them for a sitrep."

I walked off without giving them a chance to reply.

TWENTY

DESPITE EVERYTHING ELSE THAT WAS GOING ON AT THE

resort, I still didn't believe Diana Berglowe or her pearls were in any real danger. So when I—after a quick jaunt back to my villa to grab a small briefcase—found a young couple sitting on our bench with a posture that indicated they weren't leaving anytime soon, I decided to have a little fun.

"Excuse me," I said.

They both looked up from a brochure they were studying.

"I'm supposed to meet a woman here in a few minutes," I said, looking around to make sure she wasn't approaching. "Would you mind telling her to meet me in the garden instead?"

The guy furrowed his chin and nodded. "Sure."

"She's wearing a brown, flowing dress, has black hair, maybe forty. You can't miss her," I added, making sure to look at the woman as much as the man as I said it.

"No problem," the woman said.

I thanked them with a nod and headed off with a cockeyed grin on my face. My mother would not approve, but she was on the other side of the state.

The garden area has its share of flowers and ornamental shrubs and trees, including a greenhouse that's open to the public, a couple of small reflecting pools, benches and picnic tables, and plenty of open grass to walk on while pondering poetry or whatever one does in an English garden. I sat on a bench between the two pools and rested my left ankle on my right knee as I waited for Diana. My view of the stacking slider doors and the bench where we were to meet was blocked, mostly by a row of red cedars beyond the pool. Diana came through a gap in them five minutes later, hesitantly at first, then with purpose when she saw me. Her path took her around the pool and, with a few furtive glances, to me on the bench.

"Is something wrong?" she asked immediately as she sat down.

"No. I just thought we should conduct this transaction in private."

An older couple was strolling through the grass well to our left but paying us no mind.

"I have the pearls in my purse," she said, touching the bag over her right shoulder.

I reached down beside me and lifted the briefcase by the handle and set it on the bench between us. I had already unscrambled the three-digit lock, and I slid the clasp aside to crack it open. Diana swung her purse to her lap and reached into it. She pulled out a small velvet pouch, looked at me, and dropped it into the opening. Just that quickly, I clicked the briefcase shut and spun the combination.

"I'll take them back to my villa and put them in my safe immediately," I said.

"Thank you, Mr. Shades. I feel so much better."

"How long will you be staying at the hotel?"

"My flight leaves tomorrow afternoon. Might we arrange for me to get them back about the same time tomorrow?"

"Of course. If you need them sooner, I'll be around."

She nodded.

"Is there something else I can do for you?" I asked, sensing concern beyond what played on her face.

"It's the man I saw, the Arab," she said, wringing her hands.

"Did you see him again?"

"No, but I just can't shake the thought of him . . ."

"If I may, what are your plans for the remainder of your stay?"

"I've yet to take a swim in the ocean. I thought perhaps this afternoon, and then I wanted to enjoy a nice dinner at The Oak Room and a balmy evening by the pool." She smiled thinly. "It doesn't sound like much, I know."

"It sounds like a perfect way to spend a vacation," I said. "And I don't think you'll be in danger in any of those places, not without the pearls on your person."

"I hope you're right."

"I'll see if I can find anything out about your mystery man," I added.

"Thank you again, Mr. Shades."

We both stood. I offered to walk her back to the hotel, but she said she'd rather I secure her pearls. So we split up. I returned to my villa and locked Diana's pearls in the safe with Gia's cheapo sunglasses, Stewart's ledger and key, and my poker winnings. Then I poured myself half a glass of iced tea and went out onto the deck.

My lunch with Caridad hadn't confirmed any of my suspicions, nor had it alleviated any. I liked her theory that Stewart had been a broker. He had taken the sunglasses, thinking they contained the missile specs, from Gia, who Tony had used as a mule. Caridad was either the buyer who had gotten antsy and killed Stewart so as not to have to pay, only to find out he had the wrong pair of sunglasses, or she was a third party with knowledge of the transaction who had jumped him and killed him, only to find out he had the wrong pair of sunglasses. In either case, that meant she likely had the money—as the buyer who was trying to save it or as the third party who had taken it from Stewart but still wanted the specs. Or it was possible the buyer still had the money and was waiting for verification from Stewart—which he hadn't been able to provide—before making payment. That would leave Tony in a pickle, having not been paid. And it didn't account for Angelo Ravello and his pals.

There was one other wildcard, and that was Gia. I was pretty sure she was innocent in all this; the only way she wasn't was even more convoluted than the rest of my musings. And if I was going to get past musings, I had to take a chance—it was time to start playing my cards.

So I called her room, got no answer, and left her a message. I told her I needed to run a few errands, and would she like to accompany me. Then I teased about our dinner wager and asked her to give me a call back.

I waited until my tea was gone, then set out for the hotel.

TWENTY-ONE

"YOU HAVE ANY IDEA WHAT THIS MIGHT OPEN?" I ASKED

Lenny, handing him the key from Stewart's secret strongbox. We were in his office, on the first floor, behind the stairs. It was a windowless room with a bunch of TV screens on one wall that showed security footage. It was all also recorded onto video cassette tapes stored in a closet.

"Locker at a train station."

"Train station?"

"Lot of tracks, horns, tearful goodbyes."

"Good one, Lenny. I mean train station as opposed to bus station or airport."

"Nah, it's a train station locker."

Locker C12, to be precise. That narrowed down my errands later.

"Another question for you."

"Shoot."

"Know a good place around here to buy cigars?"

"Are you kidding? It's Miami."

"I mean good cigars."

Lenny lowered his face and looked at me out the top of his eyes. He cleared his throat. "Like . . . *muy bueno* cigars?"

"Like the kind I won't get arrested for buying," I said.

"Try Smokin' Joe's on Northwest 5th Street," he said.

"Thanks.

"What do you need cigars for, anyhow?"

I decided to play his own game with him. "Smoking."

"Good one, Shades."

I nodded. "You know if Summer's in?"

"Nah, she still won't let me put that camera behind her desk."

Two to one, Lenny.

"Yeah, all right. Thanks."

"Anytime, Shades."

I exited to the atrium and swept my eyes over the various seating alcoves in search of an Arab. I didn't see one, but Diana hadn't said that he was dressed like a sheik, and an Arab and a Cuban and a well-tanned, dark-haired Floridian didn't necessarily look all that different. Plus, half the people in the atrium were hidden behind ferns and fan palms. But I doubted, if Diana's mystery man actually existed, that he sat leering from behind a newspaper with two holes cut out of it anyhow. So I tried a different tack and climbed the semicircular stairs to the second floor.

Helaine looked up from her moderately-paced typing as I came in.

"Hello, Shades."

"Summer have you working all Saturday?"

"Only until three o'clock," she said, looking up at the clock on the wall. "Oh dear."

"You behind?"

"Not really. Mr. MacMillan will be watching a ball game all afternoon anyhow."

I frowned, not following her concern followed by lack thereof. "Is Summer in?" I asked.

"She is, dear."

"Can I see her for a minute?"

Helaine looked at me with a disapproving smile.

"*May* I see her for a minute?"

"I'll have to check."

Like a tortoise, she reached for her phone and punched the direct line to Summer's office. "Shades is here to see you. Do you have a minute? . . . He didn't say. . . . I can ask him." She covered the phone's mouthpiece but then uncovered it before saying anything to me. "All right." She hung up the phone at the same pace, then turned to me. "Go on in, hon."

"Thanks, Helaine."

Summer was not at her desk but standing by the window looking toward the Miami skyline. She wore the same peach, knee-length dress as that morning, now with a thin sweater to cover her bare arms.

"I interrupting?" I asked as I closed the door behind me.

"No," she said. "I needed a break anyhow. What's going on?"

"I have a couple favors to ask."

"Of course you do."

"Any word from Miami P.D.?"

"Nothing yet."

"Any guests in a dither?"

"Dither?"

I shrugged.

"Did you come here to make small talk?"

Point taken. "Miss Berglowe, the woman with the pearls, she's afraid someone was spying on her."

"Spying?"

"She said an Arab man was lurking in the lobby and watching her."

"An Arab man?"

"Even wore sunglasses inside, can you imagine?"

That at least drew an upturn at the corners of her mouth.

"You happen to know if we have any Arabs staying here this weekend?"

The upturn disappeared. "How would I know that?"

I shrugged again.

"We don't require guests to state their ethnicity or nationality."

"Any chance I can look through the guest list?"

"For what?"

"Mohammeds and Alis."

"No chance."

I sighed.

"If she's concerned, you can offer her the house safe."

"I did. She wanted something more secure."

Summer frowned.

"My safe."

"You put her pearls in your safe?"

I nodded.

"Did you give her a receipt?"

"Never crossed my mind."

"You realize she could claim you stole them."

"Why would she do that?"

"Any number of reasons. You really shouldn't have done that. It's sloppy."

I debated arguing, but not doing so was the quickest way to get out of this discussion, which was going nowhere. I did not debate telling Summer about the ledger or key, not yet anyhow.

"Is there something else?" she asked. "I needed a break, but not a long one."

"Um, yeah. Mind if I check my machine?"

She sighed but nodded toward her phone. I quickly called my answering machine and found I had a message from Gia. She was going for a swim after shuffleboard but would meet me in the atrium at three. That left nearly an hour, so I decided to do a little more sleuthing—since Summer wasn't being helpful. She couldn't help herself and raised a questioning eyebrow as I hung up the phone.

"Just confirming a date for this afternoon," I said.

She glared, and I smirked and beat a hasty retreat.

TWENTY-TWO

GEORGE OFTEN PLAYS THE BABY GRAND PIANO IN THE
atrium on weekend afternoons. He was working through some of the
classics while I waited for Gia, having spent the better part of forty-
five minutes wandering the grounds looking for anyone who
appeared to have Arabic features. I crapped out and swung by Sweet
Creams to see if anyone had pinched some taffy in my absence. Just
in case Summer remembered amid the murders and sloppy
procedure. I had just enough time to stop in my villa and put on a
fresh shirt, blue with white cuffs and collar. It matched my eyes.

Gia was late, but worth it. She wore a pink square-neck sundress
and had styled her hair down after her swim. She wore,
coincidentally enough, a silver necklace with a small strand of pearls.
High-heeled sandals gave her a couple inches of extra height, leaving
her maybe half a foot short of me. But that really wasn't on my mind.

"Cute dress," I said as I stood to greet her. "How was your swim?"

"Quiet."

I frowned.

"I went in the ocean."

"First time?"

"I live on Long Island. We can see the ocean from our house."

"First time in a *warm* ocean?"

"Ha-ha."

I was a little disappointed she didn't punch my shoulder, but I got over it. In case Summer was watching, I offered her my arm. Gia sort of liked it too, judging by the cherubic smile as she clasped it loosely in her fingers.

"Where are we running these errands?"

We started toward the front exit. "Nowhere exciting."

"Hmm."

"I'll buy you ice cream afterward."

"I had ice cream last night."

"So? You're on vacation."

"Good point."

We exited the atrium to a canopy-covered, hedge-lined, curving sidewalk that led to the terrace where the concierge, valet, and bellhops resided. The entire terrace was covered by a giant canopy and included a couple of benches set amid a virtual forest of palms and flowers, as was a small fountain stocked with goldfish. I had called before leaving my villa, asking them to have my car ready in ten minutes, and with Gia's acceptable tardiness, we didn't have to wait.

"Is that yours?" she asked, nodding at my crimson red Chevy Camaro Z28 T-Top. Two thick stripes at the bottom were white and gold, and I'd paid a guy a grand to custom paint white and gold arrowheads on either side in front of the wheels and a matching feather between the wheels, extending from the shaft of an arrow.

"Uh-huh," I said, swapping a Lincoln for the keys from Randy, one of the red-vested valets. He got Gia's door for her while I slid behind the wheel.

Gia tucked her hair behind her ear and looked my way. "I just knew you drove a cool car."

I winked and turned the ignition, and the Camaro growled to life and then purred like a jungle cat. I will never get tired of that sound, or the looks it puts on people's faces.

"So what's the story on the paint job?" Gia asked as we turned onto the two-lane road that services The Grandeur and several other hotels and resorts. A quarter mile north of the hotel, it connects to the A1A, the main north-south drag in Miami Beach.

"It mimics Florida State's helmet."

"A helmet?"

"An inverse of it, technically. It's gold."

Gia frowned. Tucked more hair behind her ear. I had to be careful not to get distracted.

"Why Florida State's helmet?" she asked. The T-Top panels were still in, but the windows were down, so she had to raise her voice.

"I grew up in Tallahassee, just as Florida State football was coming of age. I fell in love."

She nodded. I wasn't sure if she thought that was neat or dorky. Same could be said of a lot of people's reactions to the logo on the side of the car. I didn't care; I thought it was awesome.

"Can you tell me where we're going?" she asked once we had turned north on the A1A.

I reached into my pocket and came out with the locker key on a ring around my finger. I spun it a few times, then extended it to her.

"What's this?"

"According to our Chief of Security, a key to a locker at the Amtrak station in Hialeah."

"I thought you were the Chief of Security."

"I'm the Head of Security Operations. I don't know, I didn't make the titles."

"Where'd you get this key?"

"Martin Stewart's room."

Gia looked at me, mouth agape.

"Police missed it," I said.

"Doesn't say much for them."

"I thought more it said a lot for me," I said with a wink.

"You think something in there will tell us who murdered him?"

"And/or why."

"Have a working theory?"

"Yeah." I turned my head. "But you're not going to like it."

Gia frowned.

"Where did Tony get the sunglasses he gave you?"

"What?"

"Do you know where he got them?"

"Airport gift shop."

"Did you see him buy them there?"

"No. . . . He picked them up while I was reading a magazine." She shook her head. "Why?"

"I remembered something you said, about them being smudged. I looked closer, Gia. Under a blacklight, those smudges were actually very tiny numbers, letters, and lines."

She shook her head. "Numbers, letters, and lines?"

"Missile schematics. Or, a small part of them."

Gia's mouth gaped again as we coasted to a stoplight. I downshifted into neutral.

"Why would Tony—and how do you know they're missile specs?"

"I was in the Navy."

She shook her head again. "Why would Tony have sunglasses with missile specs on them? And why would he give them to me?"

"That's the part you're not going to like." The light turned green, and I shifted into first and accelerated. I looked her way. "The only reason I can think of is because he was passing them to someone and used you as a—excuse the term—mule to do so."

Gia looked at me incredulously.

"He hides your glasses or throws them away so he has a reason to 'buy' you a new pair. He also buys you a very nice hat so you'll stand out when you go to the pool. Whoever he was passing them to identifies you by the hat, waits until you go swimming, then swipes the sunglasses. You're out a cheap pair of shades but none the wiser, and Tony's golfing so he maintains anonymity."

She opened her mouth, shut it, then opened it again. "It was his idea for me to go swimming yesterday morning. I was going to read, and he suggested I do it by the pool."

I shrugged.

"Why Tony?"

"I don't know. Could be he's a middleman, a broker," I said, realizing for the first time I had just assumed Tony was the seller. "He's your brother, and I don't mean to accuse him—but . . ."

"No, Tony's a schemer and deal maker, but . . . not a sellout. That's what we're talking about here, isn't it, giving away U.S. missile technology?"

"The numbers and letters weren't in Cyrillic."

Her incredulous face gave way to a resigned sigh as I swung a left onto State Road 934, headed toward the mainland. I saw a tan sedan—a Toyota Corolla—make the turn before the light. It had been behind us since we got on the A1A.

"I have no idea who Tony does business with, but I suppose he could have gotten himself into something. And if the money was right . . ."

"Everybody has a selling point."

"But that means . . . the buyer—I can't believe I'm talking like this—has the wrong pair of sunglasses," she said.

"Yeah. And that means either the buyer paid good money for no intel or is holding payment until they get real intel."

"Which would explain why Tony seemed so upset that my sunglasses had been stolen," she said. "Because somehow he knew it was the wrong pair."

"Likely the buyer reached out to him."

"So who's the buyer?"

"Maybe Martin Stewart."

Gia's eyes widened again.

"I found your sunglasses—mine, actually—in his room."

"You think the payment is in this locker?" she asked, holding up the key.

"It's possible. Likely, in fact."

We were on the John F. Kennedy Causeway, the breeze gusting off the beautiful water of Biscayne Bay. The downtown skyline was dead ahead. The tan Corolla was still several cars behind us. For no reason, I switched lanes. It didn't follow.

"Who broke into our suite? Stewart?"

"He was dead by then."

"So it was random?"

"Or Stewart was a broker and when he didn't verify the sunglasses—"

"Because they were really yours."

"Right. When he didn't verify, the buyer came looking for them. Or," I said with another glance in the rearview as we came off the causeway onto Treasure Island, "somebody else is involved, a third party."

"Who?"

"Caridad. Cari," I added, realizing Gia may not have known her full name.

"Why her?"

"Suddenly comes onto your brother yesterday, then comes onto me last night."

"What?"

"After poker with your grandpa, she was waiting in my villa, trying to seduce me."

"Why?"

"First of all, why not," I said with a wink. "But second, I think she was hoping to get something out of me."

"Like where the real sunglasses were?"

I nodded.

"Where are they?"

"In my safe."

She sat back and looked out the window at the passing condominiums and apartments. After a minute, she turned back to me. "How do you know all this?"

"I'm a detective," I said.

"Okay, but what kind of hotel detective has a blacklight and thinks to check sunglasses for missile schematics—or, being in the Navy or not, can tell missile schematics from . . . I don't know, jet engine schematics. And this whole scheme is pretty complicated—who puts this all together?"

The causeway broke out over the water again. I turned and made eye contact with Gia. If my suspicions were right, her brother was involved in selling state secrets. Her grandpa was a former Mafia don. She herself had run errands for him. And yet, I felt I could trust her.

"That's a little complicated," I said as we approached the 79th Street West Drawbridge, "but we've got a bigger problem first."

"What's that?" she asked with a furrowed brow.

I replied as I glanced back in the rearview mirror. "We're being followed."

TWENTY-THREE

GIA GOT A FACE-FULL OF HAIR AS SHE TWISTED AROUND IN

her seat to look out the rear window. She swiped it aside and turned back to me. "The gold sedan?"

I nodded tersely.

"You can surely outrace him."

This wasn't the time to tell her that the Camaro's 5.0 liter, V-8 engine did not have the take-off or sudden speed I had anticipated when buying it off the lot two years prior. But it handled and cornered well, and there's not much chance to open it up on Miami streets—or even the interstate most times of day—anyhow. There are, however, plenty of streets on which to lose a pursuer.

"Hang on," I said, then swerved from the left lane across to the right-hand exit, drawing a blare of a horn from behind. I gunned the engine, as if I were about to race, figuring the guy on my tail might not know I couldn't anyhow. A quick glance in the mirror revealed he hadn't made the turn and had kept going west. After one side street, I hung a hard right on the second. Gia emitted a soft squeal, which hadn't been the intent but was a pleasant side effect.

She regained her composure quickly and sat up straight. "Didn't you just turn us back to the water?"

"Yep."

She looked at me. I looked in the rearview.

"It's a dead end," she said.

"Not quite," I said, turning right—the only option—at the end of the block. I was faced with the same choice a block later. We were now headed west a block north of the highway.

"Are we playing hide and seek?"

"Something like that," I said as I downshifted at the intersection I had cruised through a minute before. "I figure they'll take the first right and head north, trying to catch us when we head farther inland."

"So we double back and get behind them?"

"Something like that," I said again, punching the clutch and accelerating. A block west I had a chance to turn south and did, then back west on the highway. I had to go several blocks before I could turn south, thanks to the Little River Canal. When I finally did, on Biscayne Boulevard/Highway 1, I was confident I had lost the Corolla.

"Add that to the list," Gia said, turning back around from another glance behind us.

"List?"

"How'd you learn to drive like that?"

"I think it's pretty much standard for young males."

"I mean thinking so fast to lose a tail. You're not just a hotel detective, are you?"

"No."

"Are you even a hotel detective?"

"I am."

She was content to wait.

"The Grandeur was built in the mid-fifties, became real popular in the early-sixties, about the time the Soviets were posturing in Cuba. JFK cooled that down, to a degree, but with the Commies just across the Straits and with Miami being the cosmopolitan city that it is, it's always going to be a hotbed for espionage and illicit activity. Throw in the growing drug trade, mostly fueled by foreign cartels, and the ever-present—ahem—Mafia with its underworld connections, and, well . . ."

"Okay, so that's Miami. What about you?"

"For some reason, starting in the sixties, The Grandeur began to attract those who wished to conduct business off the radar—spies, cartels, spies, the Mob, spies."

"Why?"

I got my bearings, then hung a right on 54th Street before answering. "It's secluded, exclusive, and a previous owner might have encouraged it."

"What about the current owner?"

"He's that former C.O. I mentioned, and his daughter runs the place."

"Does she encourage it?"

"No."

"But she doesn't discourage it?"

"Hard to do and . . . somewhat complicated."

Now Gia twirled the locker key on her finger, looking out the window again, her jaw set.

"Something wrong?"

"I get the feeling you're trying awfully hard not to tell me something."

"That's because I'm not really supposed to."

She looked back.

"But, I am going to need to trust you if I'm going to make any headway this weekend."

Her eyes widened a little, waiting.

"Summer's dad, Everett Dawson, my former C.O. had connections with the CIA, and he coordinated me getting this job. Coordinated with his daughter, the fresh out of college new manager, and with the CIA."

She kept looking and waiting for more.

"I am the hotel detective, but I'm also working for the CIA to identify spies or foreign operatives, cartel drug lords or lieutenants, and so forth. Every now and again I get involved, interrupting potential deals, passing messages via back channels, and the like."

Gia pursed her lips, her brow wrinkled in thought.

"That's part of the reason The Grandeur remains an enclave for spies and secret agents and dealmakers, because the CIA doesn't want to lose a potential source of intel, through me."

"Kind of like a cop working a C.I.?"

"Kind of."

She swallowed. "So, for example, if some meathead from Long Island was going to try to get rich passing missile specs to the Soviets or . . . whoever one passes them to, you'd be tabbed to keep it from happening?"

"In theory." I shook my head. "But nobody gave me any indication such a deal was in the works. I stumbled onto it blindly."

"Hmm."

"What?"

"Just wondering if you're telling me the truth."

"Why would I lie about this after telling you everything else?'"

"Because you want me to think you came up to me yesterday because you liked my hat and not because you wanted to pump me for info."

"I came because I liked your hat, Gia," I said, turning to look her in the eye. "And because I thought you were cute."

A smile slowly broke out onto her face. "I think I believe you."

I smiled back and decided not to tell her that sometimes the feds approached me with mob-related concerns.

Because of our tail, we had taken a roundabout way, but we arrived at Miami Station in Hialeah shortly before four o'clock. It's a blocky building surrounded by pavement and tracks, not some romantic Mission-style building encircled with palms, but we weren't there for the ambiance. Plus, the clouds in the western sky were starting to darken and build, so there wasn't time for romance anyhow.

"You said you'd need my help to make any headway this weekend," Gia said as we crossed the parking lot. She still held the locker key around her index finger. "Does that mean you have a plan?"

"Still working on it."

"One where my brother doesn't spend the rest of his life in federal prison?"

"So far, he hasn't committed espionage," I said. "Just tried to."

"I guess that's something."

"I'm working on it," I said.

The station wasn't too busy on a Saturday afternoon, which was fine by me. I didn't need witnesses. We turned down the hall with vending machines, beyond the restrooms, and found a row of lockers. On cue, Gia handed me the key.

"C12," I said, eyeing it and then scanning the lockers.

"Here," she said. Not busy, the station was air-conditioned and cold, and she clutched both of her elbows in her hands, arms across her chest.

"This mean you're passing on ice cream later?" I asked as I inserted the key.

"We'll sit outside."

I nodded and opened the locker. There was a strongbox inside, maybe twice the size of the one in the planter in Stewart's room. I feared we were doomed, without another key, but the latch was loose and unlocked. I took a step back and held the strongbox in my left hand and lifted the lid with my right. It was not a wad of cash or a pouch of diamonds.

Gia leaned in. "Payment for the schematics?"

"Not exactly," I said, turning it to her. "But it does save us our next stop."

Along with a small but bulky snap lock envelope, the only other content of the strongbox was a glass-topped humidor displaying a row of Robusto cigars. Each was wrapped and printed with a logo depicting some kind of reptile in front of a shield and identifying their country of origin: Cuba.

TWENTY-FOUR

"You're quiet." Gia observed as we drove back

toward the coast.

"I'm thinking," I answered.

"You do a lot of thinking."

I had good reason.

Martin Stewart's locker at the Amtrak station had not contained stacks of Benjamins or security bonds or anything else one might use to pay for stolen missile specs, unless the going rate for state secrets was two dozen Havana Robustos. They were an odd thing to keep locked away in a humidor in a locker, a locker that could only be accessed with a key hidden in another strongbox hidden in a potted plant at a hotel. Odder still was the other item with them. Handing Gia the humidor of cigars, I had taken out the snap lock envelope, about the size for a pouch to hold a safe deposit box key, and replaced the strongbox in the locker. Wondering if we were about to be directed to another safe or locker somewhere, I had opened it and tipped it into my palm. Out had tumbled a ring, inset with an orange stone, a few small diamonds, and inscribed:

BOOKER T. WASHINGTON HIGH CLASS OF '77.

The tumblers had begun spinning in my head as we put the humidor and ring back in the strongbox, closed the locker, and returned to the car. They had continued as Gia asked questions— Was that Stewart's ring? Was it even his strongbox in the locker? What did it all mean?—that I largely blew off as I drove back to State Road 934 and turned east.

"What are you thinking?" Gia asked.

I finally looked her way. "Stewart had the sunglasses I gave you, meaning he took them from you while you swam, or took them from someone who did. Then someone killed Stewart but left the sunglasses, meaning whoever killed him did so for a completely separate reason or whoever killed him discovered that the sunglasses didn't contain the specs."

She nodded along.

"That leads me to believe that either Stewart was the buyer and someone else killed him for the specs, which he didn't have, or Stewart was a middleman—a broker of sorts. In that case, he could have been killed by the same someone else trying to horn in on the deal or by the buyer who thought he was holding out or who didn't want to pay or whatever."

"Which do you think it is?"

I briefly remembered lunch with Caridad, along with flashes of a three of clubs and a three of hearts.

"I think Stewart was a broker. I think he was supposed to grab the sunglasses, verify the specs were legit, and then make the payment."

"But pay with what? He had nothing on him, or in his locker?"

"Not yet," I said. "I think he was going to get it."

"How?"

We stopped at a light, and I rolled my head her way. "You're not going to like it."

"Now what?"

I swallowed. "Last night, after poker, the guys invited me back to play some more tonight, and Uncle Frankie asked me to supply the cigars."

"So?" Her eyes widened. "The other stop we were going to make."

"And remember what we were talking about—what you were doing—when he and Angie first found us at lunch."

She narrowed her gaze as I accelerated on green. "No, sorry, I don't."

"You had just asked me about my ring," I said, holding up my right hand. "You were holding it, in fact, gave it back to me in their presence. A little bit later, they invite me to play poker and then ask me to bring cigars the next night. Now we find Martin Stewart's strongbox containing a humidor of Cuban cigars and a class ring."

"That's awfully coincidental."

"It's more than that. I think Stewart was supposed to grab the sunglasses, verify them, and then authenticate himself to your grandpa and his gang by wearing or flashing a class ring. Maybe part two of the authentication was to provide cigars for poker night."

Gia frowned. "Wait a second. You're saying Grandpa Angie and Uncle Frankie are buying stolen missile schematics?"

"Or are brokering for someone else, maybe not even knowing what they're brokering."

"And they think you're a broker too because of your ring?"

"That was the signal to invite me to poker."

"Did they give you any payment? I mean, that's the theory, right, that they would pay Stewart—who they thought you were—after he verified the schematics, and Stewart would then somehow pay the seller?"

"In theory."

"Well, did they?"

I almost missed the next red light and had to slam on the brakes as I quickly downshifted. "No. But maybe."

She frowned.

"I cleaned them out at poker pretty good."

"They're a bunch of old guys who drink and swap stories instead of concentrating, and who can't see well enough to tell a heart from a diamond."

"You warned me not to lose my shorts."

"I was flirting."

Despite the situation, I smiled.

"How much did you clean out?"

"A couple grand."

"Seems kind of paltry for missile specs, doesn't it?"

I sighed. "It does."

"Maybe they'll up the stakes tonight."

"You're teasing me now," I said.

"Well . . ."

"There's an awful lot of coincidence otherwise," I said.

"And the alternative is that my entire family is involved in treason, my brother selling state secrets and my grandpa buying them. And why come all the way down here and involve Stewart or you and poker games and class rings and sunglasses and hats? Why not have Tony come over for some rigatoni one night and make the switch?"

I pursed my lips.

"Green."

I accelerated.

"Don't you think that's a little convoluted, all these drops and authentications and secret handshakes?"

"Unless they didn't know each other was the buyer and seller. Or didn't want the other one to know."

"I can't believe this, Shades."

I looked at her. "And yet you're not demanding that I stop so you can get out or punching my arm in a mix of yelling and crying."

"What are you saying?"

"That part of you does believe it—or, at least, believe it's possible."

She looked at me for several seconds, then drilled my arm harder than any female had ever done so. She turned and looked out the window, letting her hair swirl. And flexing her fingers.

I thought through everything again, wondering if I had jumped to a conclusion somewhere, if I had added two and two and come up with five. Speculation and guesswork, to be sure, but the math checked. Admittedly missing some of the variables, but the equation as it stood pointed to Tony and Angelo as buyer and seller, with Stewart as the middleman and me just caught in the middle.

Gia turned back, her face giving nothing away. "What about Cari? I thought you said she was involved?"

"I think she killed Stewart."

"Her?"

"Maybe she's the ultimate buyer and decided to cut out some of the middlemen. Maybe she didn't want to mess around with paying.

Or, and this is most likely, she's a third party who somehow got wind of what was going on."

"So basically the only two dupes who didn't know were me and the U.S. government."

I raised an eyebrow.

"What?"

"Yesterday, a couple of feds asked me to keep an eye on your grandpa and his pals. They said they had reason to believe something was going down, that they weren't all here in Miami to catch up and play shuffleboard. The FBI probably expected some sort of Mafia deal, not espionage, so the U.S. government had wires crossed, but wasn't entirely blind to it."

"Meaning I'm the dupe."

"I didn't say that."

She looked at me.

"And being in the dark about your family committing treason isn't a bad place to be."

Gia took a breath. "When yesterday?"

"Hmm?"

"When yesterday did these feds ask you to keep an eye on Grandpa Angie?"

"*After* I met you by the pool."

She nodded.

"Gia, if I thought you were part of this or was only hanging around you to get close to them, why would I tell you any of this?"

"I don't know."

"I wouldn't."

"So why are you telling me this?"

"Because I'm hoping you'll help me."

"Help you what, catch my brother *and* my grandpa in criminal activity—treasonous activity?"

"If we catch them and recover the specs and the payment, no harm is ultimately done. And if they agree to testify against whoever is behind this—who Tony got the specs from in the first place, who the ultimate buyer is—and if someone with a little bit of clout with the CIA calls in a few favors, they might come out of this unscathed. If we don't get involved, that doesn't happen—or worse, U.S. military specs fall into the wrong hands. I can't let that happen."

Gia pursed her lips. She finally addressed the hair that had blown into and around her face.

I coasted into another light that had just turned red.

"There are three things important to the Ravello family," she said. "One, is the family, and I mean that lowercase. Two, really good pasta. And three, this country. We have always been a family of patriots. My great, great-grandfather came here penniless but grew rich because of the American dream. I can't say that we've always achieved that dream through the best means, but we have always embraced it. Uncle Frankie fought at Anzio, for crying out loud." She shook her head. "If Tony or Grandpa Angie have betrayed that love, that patriotism, then they have betrayed our family and our history." She looked deep into my sunglasses. "If you promise me, Shades, that you will do everything you can to protect them from prison, from public embarrassment and from having the Ravello name tarnished . . . then I will help you."

"I will do everything I can, short of letting the deal go through."

She sat back. "So what do we do?"

"I'm thinking," I answered.

Gia nodded. "It's green."

TWENTY-FIVE

A SQUALL OVERTOOK US AS WE REACHED BISCAYNE BAY.

its beautiful blue surface had been turned to choppy gray as giant raindrops drummed on the window and fiberglass roof panels of the Camaro. It was cacophonous on the canopy carport, but the covering did its job and kept us dry. Spray from the wind got us a little as we walked back to the atrium, which was a hub of activity, filled with everyone who had come in from outside. Rain hitting the skylights added to the noise, and I pulled Gia close to ask, "Still up for ice cream?"

"In the rain?"

"They also have coffee and fudge."

"That could work. But how do we get there?"

"Wait until it lets up and then hurry."

"Hmm. I'm going to change into something a little warmer."

I hid a frown.

"And get a hat."

I winked. "Now you're talking. Meet me on the ground level at the far end of the hotel. Closest exit to the parlor."

She nodded and headed for the elevators.

I took the strongbox to the front desk and checked it with them. Then I walked to the far end of the hotel and watched the rain splash on the shuffleboard courts until Gia came down on the elevator. She wore bright blue-green pants and a thin white sweater open over a floral blouse. It contained the same blue-green hue as the pants, and a little bit of pink because that was apparently her color. She carried her straw hat with the white ribbon in her hands.

"What if it rains until dinner?" she asked.

"Then we squeeze in ice cream between dinner and poker. But it won't."

"How do you know?"

"Because I've lived here a while. Afternoon thundershowers are common."

She nodded.

I was proved right in five minutes when the rain dwindled to a sprinkle.

"Shall we?" I said, offering her my hand. She took it and we exited the hotel. A direct route to Sweet Creams would have meant cutting across the wet grass, so we followed the sidewalk to the vacant pool area and from there to the parlor. Aside from a few drops off palm fronds, we stayed dry. Thunder rumbled in the distance, and I couldn't tell from it or the clouds overhead if storms were coming or going. But we were safely inside again.

"Smells spectacular," Gia said, inhaling aromas of chocolate fudge and waffle cones and other fresh confections.

"Tastes even better," I said.

Brooke was working, but one of the other employees took our order, a coffee with cream and sugar and several pieces of fudge for Gia and two scoops of rocky road in a waffle cone for me. We took our snacks to a booth in the corner by a south-facing window and slid into opposite sides of the table.

Now wearing her hat, Gia leaned forward, resting her elbows on the table and cradling her coffee cup in her hands. "You have a plan yet?"

"I think so." I took a lick. "If our theory is right, our trading sunglasses yesterday morning threw a wrench into everything. Gummed up the works. Maybe got Stewart killed."

"Ouch."

I shrugged. "Purely accidental," I said and took another lick. "Worst case, in a deal like this, if the seller doesn't have legit goods, he gets—" I slid my finger across my throat.

Gia winced.

"But that hasn't happened. Tony's alive and well."

"Meaning?"

"Meaning either the buyer doesn't know he's the seller, or they're giving him a chance to recover the goods, or they walked away from the deal. Or," I said after another lick, "the wrong person was authenticated as the broker, throwing a second wrench into the deal."

"So what is the plan?"

"We take the wrenches out."

She stared at me.

I licked.

"How?"

"We don't know exactly what happened with the payment, or how it was supposed to be paid, or even what the payment is. But we do know, at least we think, how the buyer was to authenticate the broker."

"The ring and cigars and poker."

I nodded.

She finally lifted a piece of fudge off her plate. Before taking a bite, she asked, "So you go through with poker tonight?"

I nodded. "As far as Angie and the guys know, I am the broker. The problem is, they or the buyer they're working for haven't been able to authenticate the specs and thus haven't greenlit the payment. So, like I said, we remove the wrench."

She shook her head.

"We give the specs back to Tony."

Gia nearly choked on a drink of coffee.

I licked some more ice cream while she came around.

"How do we—hmm—do that?"

"You play the dingbat and say you found them at the bottom of your bag, then leave them somewhere that he can grab them. And he will, either buying you a replacement or playing you as the dingbat right back. Then he'll have to arrange to make the transfer again, only this time not using you as a mule."

"How?"

"Beats me. But he'll want to do it quick since you're leaving tomorrow, as most likely are the buyers or their brokers or whoever Angie and the guys are in this. I'll be watching and when they make the swap or transfer or whatever, I'll catch them in the act."

"That's it?" she asked.

"That's it," I said, finally getting far enough down on my ice cream to take a bite that included waffle cone.

"What if he resists?"

"I can take him," I said.

"What if he has a gun? Or Angie or Frankie do? Or what if Cari shows up again?"

"I have a gun too. But I don't think this ends with gunfire."

"No? We're talking espionage worth, what, millions? People will do anything for that kind of money."

"That's where you come in."

She dropped the piece of fudge she had just picked up. "Me?"

"For starters, you can help be my eyes and ears. I can't be everywhere at once. You keep an eye on Tony when I can't, call me if he sneaks out of the room at two a.m., that sort of thing. And if he or Angie do get me at gunpoint, you plead with them not to go through with it. Never underestimate the power of a woman's tears."

Gia tilted her head, looking at me funny.

"What?"

"An hour ago, I thought you were brilliant. Now I'm starting to wonder if you're not just a little crazy."

"The two aren't always mutually exclusive."

"What if this goes wrong? You have to admit, it's chancy, and you said you couldn't let treason actually play out."

"Sometimes you have to bet big to win big," I said.

"Why not just hang onto the specs? Then the deal's off, right?"

"Because while sunglasses with printing only visible under blacklight make a clever way to pass specs from one person to another, I doubt that's how they were leaked from a top-secret government facility. Whether it's Tony or the next guy, if the deal falls apart here, they'll try it again—somewhere that I can't intervene. This is the only chance to catch the big fish and make sure it doesn't ever happen."

Gia ate her piece of fudge and thought. I licked some more ice cream and bit off some more cone and, oddly enough, my eyes wandered from her face. They spotted a kid, maybe a teenager, maybe not yet, eying the fudge. He wore a pair of cutoff shorts and a T-shirt with a hole in it, mismatching shoes. Dark hair spilled out from under and through the hole of a backward University of Miami baseball hat. As I watched him and licked, he watched the flow of customers and especially the flow of employees. For several minutes, he lingered, and I nodded at Gia when she realized I was staring past her. She turned, and together we watched him wait for an opportunity, then sneak his hand under the sneezeguard and lift out a small tray of fudge.

That didn't surprise me; I had seen it coming. What did surprise me as I zoomed out my focus was to see Brooke watching while the kid dumped the fudge into a fanny pack as he shuffled toward the restrooms.

"Excuse me a minute," I said as I took a big bite of ice cream and cone. I stood, bided my time while two customers ordered ice cream, and then approached the counter.

"Hey, Brooke."

"Hey, Shades." She looked down. "Did you see that?"

"I did."

She swallowed. "I think he's homeless. He's been coming around the last week or so and . . . I can't find it my heart to stop him." She finally looked up. "Shades, he had a little girl with him the other day. She couldn't have been more than ten and looked just as pitiful. I was even going to put some of my money in the till as soon as I figured out a way to sneak it in there." She bit her lip, hard enough I thought it was going to bleed. "Are you going to tell Summer?"

"No," I said, reaching back for my wallet—hard while holding an ice cream cone. I managed to extract a couple of twenties. I slid them across the counter to her. "Give him a couple cookies next time too."

Her fretful face turned to a wide grin, and she nodded and pocketed the cash.

One mystery solved, I turned back to Gia. She was sitting sideways on the end of the booth seat. "Was that what I think it was?" she asked.

"Was what what?"

"Um-hmm." She smiled. "You're all right, Shades."

"I have my moments."

I slid back into the booth, and she turned to face me. "Now, if we're going to pull off this plan of yours, I want to make sure we've got all the details ironed out."

"Then let's get to ironing."

TWENTY-SIX

Gia, Tony, and I sat in a booth in the corner of the

Oak Room, dining on steaks grilled to perfection. He and I both had donned dinner jackets, mine garnet red, his likely the same blue one as the night before. Gia wore a hunter green gown that could have won her a pageant, her hair styled up with a few curls left loose beside large gold hoop earrings. They matched a heart-shaped locket that rested against her sternum on a simple chain. It caught the flickers of light from candles at the center of the table and on the wall above. (So did her eyes, but that's so prosaic.) Aside from lights on the sides of the booths to mark the aisles and a few soft white lights recessed in the ceiling, all the light in The Oak Room came from candles, creating a dark and cozy atmosphere. How I wished Tony didn't have to be there.

I was actually surprised he was. When the rain had let up again, Gia and I had left Sweet Creams and walked back to my villa. I'd given her a quick tour, then retrieved the sunglasses from my safe. She had then returned to her suite to "find" her sunglasses, notify Tony of the same, and invite him and a guest to dinner. She'd called me to confirm dinner, and also said that she'd found her sunglasses, in a way that told me he was listening. We had met up at seven-thirty, and—after I'd appropriately complimented Gia for her appearance—Tony and I had shaken hands. His face gave nothing away.

While we waited for our entrées, the three of us chatted about nothing in particular—the day's weather, a recap of Gia's shuffleboard game with Grandpa Angie, Tony's afternoon on the beach and being chased inside by storms. It was all amicable, and yet in a phony sort of way, as if we were dodging the elephant in the room.

Over salads, the conversation turned to our pasts. I talked about my time in the Navy, giving a standard spiel that revealed nothing. Gia recapped brother-sister adventures on Long Island. Tony talked business, but not in any way that hinted at how he had come to be selling missile specs. It was decent enough conversation, but again felt like fighters circling in the ring for another round.

Not until juicy, sizzling T-bones with sides of garlic mashed and scalloped potatoes and asparagus shoots were served did Gia throw what might be considered the first haymaker. "So what happened with you and Cari, anyhow?" she asked Tony as she lifted her goblet of ice water.

"Nothing much, I'm afraid."

"Don't tell me you brushed her off to mix more business and pleasure."

"No business," he said, reaching for his own drink. "She apparently lost interest."

Judging by how I'd hustled the patriarch of the Ravello family the night before, I was pretty sure my poker face gave nothing away.

He sawed into his steak. "So, Shades, any progress on the murder?"

"Nothing from the cops," I answered.

"What about you? Gia tells me you had some theories."

I covered with a bite of steak that was on my fork. I hadn't specifically told Gia not to say anything, but thought it was general common sense. I bought a little more time by clearing my throat and taking a drink after swallowing.

"Theories, but nothing more."

"Mind sharing? I find criminal investigations fascinating. I grew up watching *Kojak* and *Starsky & Hutch*."

"Grew up?" Gia said. "Weren't you already grown?"

He shushed her with a wave of his hand. "You mind?" he asked again before dipping into his potatoes.

I figured it wouldn't hurt any, so I looked right at him and said, "I think Stewart might have been a broker."

"A broker? Like a stockbroker?"

"No, like an intermediary, a third party between whom a buyer and a seller could pass goods and payment for said goods."

"Goods," he said, reaching for his water again. "What kind of goods?" he asked before drinking.

"That I don't know. Could be anything from jewels, antiques, drugs—which are ever-present in Miami—other illicit materials. No idea."

"No foolin'? What makes you think he was a broker?"

"He frequented the hotel, always the same room, and I found a locker key hidden there."

"You did?"

I nodded.

"What kind of locker?"

"Don't know. Gia and I ran out to the Amtrak station this afternoon," I said, glancing at her, hoping she could keep up a good cover. "Nothing there."

"Nothing? You found the locker?"

I nodded.

"And it was empty?"

I nodded again.

"Strange."

"Not if he was waiting to make a deal when he got popped. Or had just finished it."

"And no idea who killed him?"

"No," I said.

He looked down and took a bite, and I looked at Gia again. Her face, as was the night's theme, revealed nothing.

"So that's where you were this afternoon?" Tony said, looking now to her. I decided to get back after my steak.

"That and a swim, shuffleboard with Grandpa Angie."

I thought Tony might have been getting suspicious, but he broke into a smile. "And you mock me for watching detective shows."

"Truth be told, Tony, I just invited her along without telling her where I was going."

"You two are spending a lot of time together," he said, pointing at us non-threateningly with his steak knife.

"We are," Gia said. She reached out her left hand and placed it on mine. I looked at her, then at Tony.

"Well, frankly, it's about danged time, Gia. I can't remember the last guy who spiked your meter. I'm telling you, Shades, this girl would rather stay in and read a book or cook a meal for her grandpa than go out on a date."

"I'm just selective," she said.

Tony was about to argue when the maître d' approached our table. "Excuse me, sir," he said, looking at me. "There's a telephone call for you."

I dabbed my mouth with a napkin, excused myself, and followed him through the restaurant. Instead of directing me to the pay phone by the hallway to the restrooms, he gestured to a black phone that was off its cradle behind the maître d' desk. I thanked him and picked it up. "This is Shades."

"Shoot, I forgot a codename," Kevin said.

"Hey, what's up?"

"I talked to Eileen at the gift shop. She said a guy matching Tony's description came in and bought a pair of cheap sunglasses about seven tonight."

I smiled. He'd taken the bait.

"What kind?"

"Real crappy ones, man, dark lenses, plastic stems. You know the type."

I did indeed. Just like the original pair he'd bought Gia, the kind available in every gift shop in every resort or airport in the world.

"You need anything else from me tonight, man?"

"You have somewhere to be?"

"Not exactly, but I wasn't planning on running errands for you on a Saturday night."

"I'll make it worth your while."

"Put in a good word with Brooke for me?"

"Not that worth your while. Come on, Kev, you know I'll make it right."

He sighed. "What do you need?"

"Put on something resort-like, nondescript, and come keep an eye on a guy for me."

"Are you for real?"

"I am."

Kevin sighed again.

"I'll maybe invite Brooke to your birthday bash next month."

"Deal. What am I watching for?"

"Anything suspicious." I gave him a few more details, made him give me some on what he determined to be nondescript resort wear, and then confirmed times. Then I headed back to the table.

"Everything all right?" Tony asked.

"Yeah. That was my boss, had questions about a petty theft case I'm looking into for her."

Then, to keep the subject off anything else, Gia and I told him about the kid who had been stealing from Sweet Creams and Summer's obsession over nickels and dimes.

We finished dinner, passed on dessert, and then Tony and I fought over the check. I ended up winning. More like he ended up losing on purpose after a fake fight.

"You two have plans for the evening?" he asked as we exited The Oak Room, into a hallway that serviced both it and The Coconut Grille. We turned and walked slowly toward the exit.

"He does," Gia said wistfully, having taken hold of my arm.

"Taking your grandpa and his friends for some more poker money," I said.

Tony's eyes actually widened. "You're beating them?"

"At least last night."

"Beginner's luck," he said.

I shrugged.

"Don't expect it to continue. Those guys are sharks."

We exited through sliding glass doors into a balmy, breezy evening. The rain of the afternoon was long gone, and the fresh air was invigorating.

Tony stopped at the first sidewalk intersection. He extended a hand. "Thanks for dinner, Shades."

"My pleasure."

He leaned over and gave Gia a peck on the cheek. "I'll leave you kids to it," he said with a grin, then shuffled off along the well-lit path to the atrium. I had expected as much and had told Kevin to pick him up there. It was fifty-fifty if Tony would spot him as a tail and lose him or just lose him accidentally, but it was worth a shot.

Gia and I lingered slowly. When Tony was out of earshot, she said, "Well?"

"He bought you new shades. Probably going to make the switch right now."

"And then make a deal?"

"At some point."

"I guess I should go keep an eye on him," she said, dropping my arm.

"If he goes to make a deal, he'll probably try to leave you behind."

"Then I'll hide in the shadows."

"Might want to change first," I said with a sly grin. "You're kind of conspicuous."

She slapped my arm playfully.

"I also brought in my friend Kevin, to keep an eye on him." I described what he was wearing. "In case you two need to tag-team."

"This is kind of fun. I just wish it wasn't my brother and grandfather."

"Remember, if we can keep them from making the deal, I think we can keep them out of trouble. Major trouble, at least."

She nodded.

"I should get running," I said.

"Will you call me after the poker game?"

"It might be late."

"I'll be up, either watching Tony or . . . waiting to hear from you."

"I'll call you," I said.

She took a step closer. "Will I see you again before . . . before we leave tomorrow?"

"Of course."

"I mean, other than if we make a bust or something?"

"Yes. I promise."

"Then I'll save your goodbye kiss for later."

She smirked, and I couldn't help return it as she turned and strode off toward the atrium.

TWENTY-SEVEN

THE QUICKEST WAY BACK TO MY VILLA WAS THROUGH THE

edge of the English garden, via a patio known as the square. Surrounded by eight-foot hedges except where the sidewalk led in and out, the patio features a large fountain, a couple seating areas, and for no reason at all, four white Georgian columns that support nothing. Soft, solar-powered spotlights at the base of the columns light them at night, and create shadows across the rest of the patio.

The shadows explained why I didn't see Caridad until I was almost upon her.

"Hello, Shades," she purred, rising from one of the benches. She wore a tight, short black dress that would have worked very well for her in the downtown club scene. In fact, it worked pretty well in a poorly lit English garden. Her hair was down, falling on bare shoulders exposed by the off-the-shoulder neckline of the dress. She took several steps toward me in stiletto heels.

"Cari, what are you doing here?"

"Waiting for you," she said. "I thought I might catch you *before* you made plans tonight."

I exhaled, and her hand paused on the lapel of my jacket. It was just light enough out for me to see her eyes widen.

"I've got plans in a few minutes."

Caridad dropped her hand. "With her?"

"Gia? No, not with her."

"Then cancel them."

"I can't."

"Or won't?"

"Dealer's choice."

She frowned.

"I'm sorry, Cari, but I do have to get going."

She was not to be so easily dissuaded and took hold of my arms. "What about after? You are not bushed tonight, are you?"

I'm a decent-enough looking guy, young, with a great head of hair. I've had women come onto me before, but never with the insistency of Caridad. In any other circumstance, I would have found it flattering, and perhaps impossible to resist. But given the fact she was my leading candidate for Stewart's murder, I couldn't bring myself to believe this was an innocent appeal. But neither could I afford, based on that lack of innocence, to blow her off entirely.

"Come on, Shades. We don't have to do anything but talk."

I gave her an incredulous look.

"I mean it. We'll have a drink, we'll talk, and you can tell me to leave whenever you want."

"We'll just talk," I said. *While you're in that dress?* "Talk about what?"

She shrugged, then crawled her fingers up my arm. "Whatever. Your day, my day, life."

"Why?"

Caridad licked her lips. "Because I like you, Shades, and I want to spend time with you."

She almost got me. She almost made me believe there was nothing on her mind but infatuation. But her quick change from seduction to conversation told me she was prying. "Your day, my day" would involve a murder investigation, her way to see what I knew. If I wasn't up for pillow talk where I might reveal something, maybe I'd do so in a late-night heart-to-heart.

"I'm afraid it's going to run pretty late tonight," I said, "but what about breakfast tomorrow?"

"If that's the best I'm going to get."

"Afraid it is tonight."

"My place or yours?"

"Well, I'm fresh out of eggs. How about The Coconut Grille?"

"How about room service on my balcony?"

I reasoned I could always jump if she tried to seduce me again. Or strangle me with a bedsheet. "Okay, nine o'clock tomorrow."

She slid her hand down my lapel and turned to go. I stood there listening to the fountain bubble for a minute, wondering if I should have made plans for tonight and stood her up, so she'd be out of the way when Tony's potential deal went down. Speaking of, it was about time for a literal and perhaps figurative deal with Angie and the boys, so I turned and headed for my villa.

I only made it halfway. Summer met me on the sidewalk coming from the villas.

"There you are," she said, as if I'd been playing hooky. "Come with me."

"Um . . . I've got an appointment," I said.

"She'll wait. I've caught a thief."

"You caught a thief?"

"Snuck behind the bar and was filling a backpack with peanuts and pretzels."

"Want me to call SWAT?"

"Make jokes if you want, but as Head Security Officer, you ought to take this more seriously."

"What did you do with this thief?"

"He's in my office, with Gerald."

Gerald was one of the security guards, one who often got stuck working graveyard shifts. No-nonsense, a really good scowling face, but that was appropriate for a late-night security guard. Terrifying, probably, for a twelve-year-old kid, assuming our taffy and fudge artist had moved on to nuts and pretzels.

"Come on," Summer said, starting past me.

"What do you want me to do?"

"Your job."

"Sounds like you already did."

She sighed. "The kid won't say a word. I'm hoping you can get through to him and see who put him up to this. You do have a strange way with children."

I wasn't sure how to take that remark, but I let it pass. "What makes you think someone put him up to it?"

"Because a kid doesn't think to steal food from behind a bar unless someone plants the idea in his head."

That was reasonable, I supposed. I checked my watch.

"This won't take long, and you can still make your date."

I didn't bother to correct her, figuring the quickest way through this mess was to humor Summer. So I followed her back past the oak tree, through the atrium, and up to her office where Gerald and the same young kid from the parlor stood practically at attention. I nodded at Gerald, then pulled out one of the chairs from in front of Summer's desk. "Have a seat," I said to the kid. He hesitated, and I nodded toward it.

Slowly, he sat.

I pulled out the other chair and sat facing him. Up close, he was maybe ten at most.

"My name is Shades," I said.

He frowned a little, but didn't answer.

"Kind of a weird name, isn't it?"

He nodded.

"I'm going to guess . . . you look like a Billy to me."

He shook his head.

"Not Billy. Maybe a Jack? No, not a Jack," I said as he shook his head. "Your name isn't Shades too, is it?"

"I'm Freddie."

"Freddie," I said with a nod. "Freddie, are you hungry?"

His brown eyes turned into dinner plates, and he gave a small nod.

"You have a sister, Freddie?"

Another nod.

"She's hungry too?"

Another nod.

"Freddie, this nice lady here is going to buy you supper, okay. And she's going to buy you something to take home to your sister too. But I just want to ask you a couple questions first."

"Okay."

"I'm not going to get you in any trouble."

I sensed Summer starting to object out the corner of my eye, but shushed her with a quick flit of my eyes. "But I do need you to tell me the truth, all right?"

Another nod.

"Have you been stealing candy from the ice cream shop?"

Freddie's lip trembled for a moment. "Y-yes."

I nodded. "And peanuts and pretzels from behind the bar?"

"Yeah."

"Did you do it because you were hungry?"

"N-n-not ex—not exactly."

"Then how come?"

He looked to Summer and Gerald, then to me. "A lady gave me twenty dollars. She said if I took some candy and some peanuts and some things from the store, she'd give me another twenty. My mom, she works two jobs and isn't around much, and sometimes she's not even home to make us supper. I can buy a lot of food for forty dollars."

"What did this lady look like?"

Freddie shrugged.

"Was she short or tall, fat or thin?"

"Not either, really."

"Dark hair, light hair?"

"Dark."

"Long?"

"It was in a ponytail. Kind of long."

"Was she pretty?"

"Sort of," he said. "She was kind of old."

"Older than her?" I said, nodding at Summer. Summer isn't old, but I needed to gauge a ten-year-old's frame of reference.

"Yeah, I think so." He tilted his head to the side. "She had a butterfly on her shirt."

"A butterfly?"

"A big gold one, like a . . ." He tapped his chest.

"A broach?" Summer asked.

"I guess."

I guessed if we spotted a youngish, sort of pretty woman with a butterfly broach, we might be onto something. "How long ago did she give you this twenty dollars, Freddie?" I asked.

"A few days. Maybe a week."

I nodded. "I'm going to talk to this nice lady for a minute, okay."

He nodded.

I stood and pulled Summer aside.

"What are you doing?" she asked.

"Trying to figure out who set this kid up."

"And having me buy him dinner?"

"What, I ruin *your* date?"

She sighed.

"I'm going to pay him off," I said.

"What?"

"Somebody paid him forty bucks to steal. We'll give him dinner for two and fifty bucks not to steal."

"What kind of message is that to send to a kid?"

"The kind that can get delivered quickly and nips your problem in the bud. Your words, I think."

She sighed.

"Unless you want to turn a hungry kid trying to feed his sister in to the cops."

"No, of course not."

"You can pay me back later," I said. "Take the cost of dinner out of your half."

Without giving her a chance to object, I returned to my seat opposite Freddie. I leaned forward. "I'll make you a deal, Freddie."

He looked at me, brown eyes still wide.

"I'll give you fifty dollars not to steal from this hotel or anybody else again."

His eyes nearly popped out of their sockets.

"But you have to promise me."

"I promise."

I extended my hand. He looked at it.

"Where I come from, men shake hands to make a promise. And it sounds, Freddie, like you're the man of your house."

He tentatively reached out and shook my hand, his eyes still wide and incredulous. They got wider when I pulled three twenty-dollar bills from my wallet.

"Guess it's sixty," I said.

"I can get fives and tens," Summer said. I started to object to her stinginess as she moved toward her desk. "Sixty dollars of fives and tens. Easier to spend."

I leaned forward and smiled at Freddie. "Make sure she buys you dessert too."

TWENTY-EIGHT

I WAS TWENTY MINUTES LATE TO POKER, AFTER RUNNING

back to my villa to get cash and cigars. Fortunately, no more women were waiting to talk to me.

"We thought you'd stood us up," Angie said when I entered the Gene E. Lowry Card Room.

"My boss had to talk to me, and then I had to run back to my villa and get these," I said, holding up the humidor of Cuban cigars.

Angie's eyes widened. "Here we go, boys," he said, taking the humidor to the bar on the side wall, next to the liquor. He drew out five cigars. "Let's try them out," he said, passing one to everybody.

The four former mobsters puffed up, and I joined in last. Soon the air was filled with a blue-gray cloud and the scent of wood and toasted almonds. I'd never seen a group of guys take to a smoke like this foursome, smiling and inhaling as if they'd never had such a pleasure. For what it was worth, I enjoyed the cigar too, but I couldn't say that particular stogie was head and shoulders better than anything else I'd ever smoked. Then again, I was here under the impression that a humidor of Cuban cigars might have been the broker's way of completing his authentication to Angie and company. For all I knew, satisfied smiles and oohs and ahs were their way of recognizing the broker.

"What do you say," Frankie said between puffs, "let's play some poker."

The guys turned toward the table, slapping my back and offering handshakes. Vinny plied me with a rocks glass. "Four horsemen," he said.

I nodded and took the open seat, same one as the night before. All of us were in the same order, and Angie again began the deal. Like the night before, I let the game come to me. I also let the conversation spin. If I was right, and I had authenticated as the broker, I'd be getting a large payment—much larger than my poker winnings. But whether that would be tonight or some other time, I didn't know. Or, for that matter, if there was more encoded vernacular to further authenticate myself.

The first several hands were anticlimactic. The guys loved the cigars, and they seemed to bring out more stories of the good old days. Once again, those stories failed to incriminate anyone. Instead, they laughed about failed romantic endeavors, fights in bars and at ballgames, and a dispute with the city's snowplowing union. Once again the conversation took the edge off. Or maybe it was the Beam, Cuervo, Daniels, and Walker.

Vinny dealt the fifth hand, and Angie led off the betting. "Twenty."

There were several intakes of breath and at least one saint named.

"You're up to something," Nicky said, and tossed in two blue chips.

Frankie muttered something in Italian and slid in his cards.

"I'm game," I said, and Vinny did likewise. Eighty bucks in the pot, plus the antes.

"I'm good," Angie said.

"Two," Frankie said.

I looked at my three kings, a six, and a five. Smart play was to take two cards, two chances to get the fourth king. But that would suggest to Angie that I only had three of a kind or three-fifths of a straight or a flush. So I took one, sacrificing the six. Vinny slid me a nine of clubs, useless, and took three cards.

Angie looked at me. "Fifty."

Nicky whistled. Then folded.

Frankie actually turned away from the table.

I looked at Angie. His left eyebrow was twitching like he'd come in late with lipstick on his collar.

"Fifty," I said, counting the chips, "and a hundred more."

Nicky whistled again. Vinny couldn't fold quickly enough.

Angie took a puff on the cigar, then clamped his lips on it. His words were distorted as he said, "See your hundred and raise you five hundred more."

The former don was either bluffing or about to have a stroke. Hoping he hadn't been made aware of his tell, I began stacking up chips. "Call."

"Jacks," he said, turning over a pair, "and nines."

"Kings," I answered, "but more of them."

"Agghh," he growled, then coughed, then sucked on his cigar.

"Angie, you old fart, you raised five hundred on two pair?" Nicky asked.

"You raised fifty on two pair?" Frankie asked.

"Agghh. I thought I'd figured out his tell."

"I don't have a tell, gentlemen," I said, raking in the chips.

"So it would seem," Vinny said.

"Refill anybody's drink?" I asked, standing with my glass.

"I'll get it, I'll get it," Nicky said and rose too. "It's a good thing you don't manage your commercial enterprises like you play cards, Angie."

"Bah," he said with a dismissive wave.

"Kid, these are the best cigars I've ever smoked," Nicky said, reaching for a snifter of cognac. "You mind if I have another?"

"Smoke 'em all," I said.

You'd have thought the Yankees or the Reds or the Twins had knocked in a couple of runs from the cheer that went up from the table, and Nicky took the humidor back as if revealing the spoils of war. I was the only one to pass on a second stogie as we began playing again. I broke even once more around the table, then was dealt a full house that won a couple hundred and three queens on the hand after that.

"Shades—where'd that name come from anyhow?" Frankie asked as I bet ten bucks.

"From his fancy shirts," Vinny said, matching my ten. "Where do you think?"

"I thought maybe because he was a hotel dick, peeking in keyholes and around the shades," Nicky said.

"Call," Angie added.

"I don't do that kind of work."

"This place is too exclusive for that," Angie added.

"Ten," Nicky said with a shrug.

"Ten," Frankie said. "Shades, how many cards?"

"A pair."

He slid them to me, two to Vinny, one to Angie, one to Nicky, and three for himself. I waited until all had been dealt, then said, "I wear sunglasses all the time because of light sensitivity. It's also why I hang out in smoky, poorly lit card rooms," I added with a wink. "Twenty-five."

"Surprised you don't wear 'em while you're playing," Vinny said. "I fold."

"No need. I've got nothing to hide."

"Reminds me of you as a youngster, Angie," Frankie said.

"Run, kid, that's trouble," Nicky said with a laugh.

Angie folded, and Nicky tossed in twenty-five. "I'll call. You fold again, Frankie?"

"Not so fast, Marino. Twenty-five and another twenty-five."

"Hey, hey, you finally deal yourself something better than a pair?"

"Another twenty-five to find out. Angie, what was the name of that guy from South Jersey who always wore sunglasses, even inside?"

"Jimmy Marcone?"

"Yeah, yeah, Jumpin' Jimmy. Wasn't he the guy who got sent up for knifing a couple of guys in a pawn shop?"

"I heard about that," Vinny said. "Maybe ten years ago? These two doofuses come in and browse for like an hour, won't buy nothing, and he finally lost it?"

Angie shook his head. "No, they contacted every pawnshop in the tri-state area, looking for—what was it, a grandfather clock? And when they finally found a guy—Jumpin' Jimmy—who could locate it and who called 'em, *then* they came and hemmed and hawed for an hour. And he kept prodding them and finally lost it and stabbed the both of them. Served a nickel at Trenton."

"This is fascinating," Nicky said. "What do you say, Shades?"

"I'm in," I said, dropping my chips in the pot.

"And I see the twenty-five and raise another fifty." He looked at Frankie. "You and your pair want out now?"

"I'll call."

"What about you, Jumpin' Jimmy?"

I leaned toward Vinny. "Which are higher again, the reds or the blacks?"

Vinny grinned. "It all depends on their shape."

"Aw, knock it off," Nicky said.

I smirked. He was bluffing, I knew, because getting angry and impatient was another tell. And because these old guys were lousy at luck and bluffed almost every hand. But I decided to let him off easy and called instead of raising some more.

"Four, five, six, seven, eight," Nicky said. He put the stub of his cigar in his mouth. "All black," he added with a sarcastic tone as we leaned in closer to confirm the five and six were clubs, but the others were spades. A straight, good but not great.

"I got a pair all right," Frankie said. "A pair of tens," he said.

"A pair of tens?" Angie said. "You do know how this game is played, don't you?"

"Tens," Frankie said, laying out the ten of diamonds and ten of clubs. "And tens," he said, laying out the ten of spades and the ten of hearts. "A pair, plural, of tens, plural."

Nicky spoke Italian, but I recognized a curse when I heard one.

After a pair of grand reveals, I followed suit, pun not intended.

"Four diamonds," I said, dropping the red-specked card. "One for each lady's finger," I said, then laid down four queens.

"Agghh," Frankie, slapping down his remaining card.

"Don't look at me," Angie said. "You dealt him the cards." He looked at me as I scooped in my winnings yet again. "Well, what do you say, Shades? That about enough?"

I looked at the clock, saw it was quarter after eleven. I looked at my rocks glass, empty. I looked at the smoldering ashtrays on the table. And I looked at four somewhat somber faces, for the first time that night. I decided not to press my luck.

"Bad form for the winner to call it a night," I said. "If you gents want more opportunity to win your money back, I'm game. But I'm more than content to walk away if you're all played out."

Angie nodded and looked around the table. He got three more nods.

"Shades, it's been a pleasure," he said, standing. He offered me a hand across the table.

"Same here, Angie," I said. "If you guys ever come back to The Grandeur . . ."

"Oh, we'll be back."

I shook hands with the rest of the guys, pocketed my cash, and then decided to make their day. "Keep the extras," I said with a nod at the humidor.

"You're a real ace," Vinny said, shaking my hand again.

"I sense you'll have much better luck in life than Jumpin' Jimmy," Frankie said with a pat on the shoulder.

I shook Nicky and Angie's hands again, then, figuring I had given them every opportunity to pay me or arrange a drop or whatever might be in the works, said goodbye and was the first through the French doors to the clubhouse lounge. At almost eleven-thirty, it was dark, just a few all-night lights over the bar and red exit signs by the doors. As a result, I didn't see Gia until she called my name.

TWENTY-NINE

TECHNICALLY, I STILL DIDN'T SEE HER UNTIL SHE SAT UP
from the couch on the left. She blinked a few times and yawned. "What time is it?"

"Past your bedtime, apparently. Eleven-thirty or so. What are you doing here?"

Gia glanced at the doors to the card room. "Walk with me?"

"Okay."

She stood and led the way out the side exit, to the portico where we had listened to the rain after tennis the previous afternoon. Instead of turning right on the sidewalk toward the main path or going straight to the tennis courts, she turned left. I followed her onto the grass, taking deep breaths of the cool night air, a refreshing change after the smoky card room.

"How was poker?" she asked. She had changed from her gown, obviously, into the outfit she'd worn to ice cream earlier. Even with the sweater, she cradled her arms in her hands.

"Good," I said. "For me."

"Did you take all those poor old men's money?"

"I took money, but I didn't see any poor men in there."

There was just enough ambient light for me to see her smile.

"Wasn't I supposed to call you?" I asked.

"You were," she said as we turned south. A brick wall to our right marked the bounds of the property and muted passing traffic on the service road outside the resort. It was surrounded by a variety of palm trees, which also blocked any chance anyone still in the card room had of seeing us.

"Something happen?" I asked.

"I went straight back to our suite after dinner. Tony was on the phone, in his room, and I couldn't hear what was said. I changed and poured myself a drink, and that soon he said he was heading out to stretch his legs. I offered to come with him, but he said he wanted to be alone, which I thought was odd."

I didn't like where this was going and was already wondering if Kevin had been able to keep tabs on Tony.

"I didn't want to be seen following him," Gia continued, "so I waited a couple minutes and then went to stretch *my* legs, figuring if he saw me, I had a legit excuse. I couldn't find him. I spent half an hour walking all over the resort, and finally gave up and came back. That's when I saw your friend, Kevin, pretending to read a book in the atrium."

"Pretending?"

"He had it upside down," she said. "He was wearing what you said he would, and I approached him and told him who I was. He said Tony had gone to the greenhouse in the garden, spent about five minutes inside, and then another five outside, like he was waiting for someone. But nobody showed, and then he walked back to the atrium and got on an elevator. So I went back to the room too."

We had reached the corner of the property, beyond the sand volleyball court, and turned east.

"Did he buy that you just went for a walk too?"

"I don't think he even noticed," she said. He was pacing and making phone calls, and finally dragged the phone out onto the balcony. He didn't know I had cracked my bedroom window earlier, so I was able to hear what he said." She looked right at me. "They're making the swap tomorrow."

My eyebrows rose.

"It sounded like someone had been planning to meet him in the greenhouse, but didn't show, so they rescheduled for the morning."

"You know when and where?"

"Seven-thirty, on the pier."

"This pier?" I said, pointing toward the beach, "the pier right down the beach?"

"As far as I know."

"You know how it's going down? Just a simple handoff, some kind of swap, a third party involved?"

"No, but it sounded like he was receiving instructions."

I placed my hand over my mouth, then slowly swiped it down over my chin.

"What are we going to do?" Gia asked. We had turned again, walking on concrete between the sand volleyball court and the basketball court, both of which were empty, well after the resort rules permitted noisy sports.

"I'll be at the pier," I answered.

"They'll see you."

"I'll be in disguise."

"As what?"

"It's a fishing pier," I said. "I'll fish."

"And what do I do?"

"You any good at taking pictures?"

"Point and click, isn't it?"

"Don't forget zoom."

"I don't have a camera."

"I do. I'll get it to you—better yet, I'll stash it, behind the umbrella box just down the beach from the property. There's a couple dunes, seagrass, some short palms—you can hide there and take pictures of everything."

She stopped and grabbed my arm. "Shades, is this going to work?"

"Better than I thought. We have advance warning of when and where the swap is going down. It'll work."

"You make it sound so easy."

"Sometimes it is," I said with a smile.

"If you say so."

"You should get back and get some sleep," I said. "I should get some sleep. We've got an early morning."

She nodded and we resumed walking, back around the south side of the clubhouse and to the main sidewalk. The lights in the clubhouse were out, so I figured Angie, Frankie, Nicky, and Vinny had left and were in bed dreaming about their marvelous cigars. In fact, I saw no one else out on the grounds, now at nearly midnight.

We stopped just outside the atrium, and Gia again took my arm. "You'll do everything you can for Tony and Grandpa Angie?"

"I will," I said, not able to avoid frowning.

"Something wrong?"

"No. I promise."

She smiled sweetly, leaned up to kiss my cheek, and then turned and went inside.

I turned back toward my villa, frowning again. If Angelo Ravello had been using a broker—one I had accidentally authenticated as—to buy missile specs from his grandson, why hadn't he done anything to initiate or schedule a payment to the assumed broker? Why wasn't the assumed broker part of the scheduled swap the following morning? And how had it been scheduled by Angie while he'd been playing poker with the assumed broker?

There were too many possible answers to too many questions, and I needed to figure them out before seven-thirty the following morning. But there were two problems. First, I was ready to crash after another long, crazy, mentally stressful day. Second, for the second night in a row, I returned to my villa to find someone waiting for me.

THIRTY

"**L**AST NIGHT'S GUEST WAS MUCH BETTER LOOKING." I

said after a taking a few seconds for my heart to start beating. I also pocketed the note that had been taped to my door, my name on it, in Kevin's handwriting if I was right. But that was a backseat priority right now.

Special Agents Costa and O'Connor both stood from the couch. They had not started a fire nor, I presumed, opened a bottle of wine.

"How did you guys get in here?"

"Your door was unlocked," Costa said.

I'd left in such a hurry with my cigars and money that I couldn't call their bluff.

"There's a difference between unlocked and open."

"Maybe, but we didn't want to alarm your neighbors if they saw us lurking."

"What do you guys want?"

185

"Isn't it obvious," O'Connor said. "How was poker with the Felonious Four?"

"Uneventful."

"Have you made any progress?"

I walked over to the bar and poured myself a glass of cognac, as I had the night before. Instead of sitting down in my rocking chair, I wandered over to the spinet piano in the corner. I set the glass on the lid—Mom would not approve—and sat down. One-handed, I began tinkling out a simple tune. It helped me think, the activity in one part of my brain freeing up another.

"Mr. Pulaski, it's late. Would you mind—"

Still playing, I turned my head. "I don't think they're up to anything. Not really, I mean."

"Not really?" Costa asked.

I sighed, still trying to figure it out for myself. It wasn't coincidence that Stewart had had, in his strongbox at the Amtrak station locker, a class ring and a humidor of cigars. That *had* to have been the reason the "Felonious Four" invited me to poker, because they thought I was the broker. But they hadn't done anything or said anything to interact with the broker. Unless . . . "it was a distraction."

"Excuse me?"

Could the poker game have been a distraction? Per Gia, Kevin had followed Tony to the greenhouse—to an exchange that didn't go down, for some reason. Had Angie and company identified me as whoever they thought Stewart was, and invited me to play poker and then invited me back to keep me—that is, Stewart—out of the way? But why not just invite me to Saturday night's game? Had something gone down—or been supposed to go down Friday too? And who was Stewart that they had to try to get him out of the way?

"Mr. Pulaski," O'Connor said.

I took my hand off the keys and reached for my glass. "Sorry, guys, but . . . I don't have anything for you."

"What's the matter," he said, stepping around the couch, hands in his pockets, "they get to you?"

I slowly took a drink and set my glass back down. "They did not *get* to me. We played poker, had a few drinks, smoked a couple cigars."

"Not Cubans, I hope," Costa said.

"I didn't ask. But if that's the worst you've got them for . . ."

"Something else?"

"No," I said, playing again, with both hands.

O'Connor came over and leaned on the piano. "I think you're hiding something, Pulaski."

I turned to him. "I think that is a baseless accusation by someone who entered my premises without permission. You want to play a game of technicality hardball, say when and where."

"There's no need to get hostile," Costa said. "Tim, come on," he said, pulling his partner's elbow. I took a drink, still playing with the right hand.

"Mr. Pulaski, have you heard anything more about Mr. Stewart's death? Any reason to believe *it* might be connected to Ravello or the others' presence here?"

"No," I said. "I've heard nothing." I sighed. "And I mean it, guys, I think you had bad intel. Whatever you thought they were up to, I think they were here to catch up, swap stories, and lose a few grand in poker hands."

"A few grand?"

"I got good cards."

"All right, we'll let you get some rest."

"You'll call us if you should learn anything more?" O'Connor asked.

"I will call you," I said, then played piano until the door closed. I stopped mid-note and hurried to the peephole to make sure they were gone. Then I bolted the door, locked the slider to the deck, and went into my closet safe.

Thoughts and words were running through my head.

By my own admission, Angie, Frankie, Nicky, and Vinny *hadn't done anything or said anything to interact with the broker.*

"We . . . smoked a couple cigars."

"Not Cubans, I hope."

Angie looked at me as I scooped in my winnings yet again. "Well, what do you say, Shades? That about enough?"

"I sense you'll have much better luck in life than Jumpin' Jimmy," Frankie said with a pat on the shoulder.

They were bumping around and colliding in my brain while I tried to sort out which were relevant and not. In the meantime, I carried Stewart's ledger and Friday night's poker winnings out to the coffee table. I added the winnings still in my pocket to them, which also reminded me of Kevin's note. I opened it.

Followed your guy to the greenhouse. He went inside for five minutes, then waited outside for five minutes, then went back to the hotel. Never saw him talk to anybody else, and I don't think he saw me. Check with your girlfriend, she might know more.

-Kev

Nothing new there, so I turned my attention back to the items on the table. Before I sat down, I remembered my cognac and went over to get it. Then I got to work.

I flipped to the last page of the ledger that had writing on it.

Boots – Piggies – 5

Cincy – Minnie – 250

Arnold – Lucy – ⏚

I sorted out the money, mostly hundreds, stacking it into piles of thousands. There were four, plus another stack that totaled $840.

Boots – Piggies – 5

I assumed that was 5k, or five grand. I thought back to my conversation with Gia on the way back from Hialeah.

"Did they give you any payment? I mean, that's the theory, right, that they would pay Stewart—who they thought you were— after he verified the schematics, and Stewart would then somehow pay the seller?"

"In theory."

"Well, did they?"

I almost missed the next red light and had to slam on the brakes as I quickly downshifted. "No. But maybe."

She frowned.

"I cleaned them out at poker pretty good."

"They're a bunch of old guys who drink and swap stories instead of concentrating, and who can't see well enough to tell a heart from a diamond."

"You warned me not to lose my shorts."

"I was flirting."

Despite the situation, I smiled.

"How much did you clean out?"

"A couple grand."

"Seems kind of paltry for missile specs, doesn't it?"

I took a drink and sat back, thinking. Five grand—or $4,840—was nowhere near enough payment, not even a down payment, for stolen U.S. military technology. But was it too much for some illegally imported Cuban cigars—*"the best cigars I've ever smoked"*? Cigars they had more or less asked me to bring when we'd finished playing Friday night? Was that the reason these former mobsters had been so bad at poker, had bluffed and had raised with lousy hands?

No, that didn't fit. A hair under five grand was way too *much* for a single humidor of Cuban cigars, best ever or not. I yawned. Then took another drink, remembering I had to be on stakeout duty by zero-seven-thirty in the morning.

On a whim, I leaned forward and picked up one of the hundreds. I held it to the light, and it passed muster. I picked up several more, for no reason, and held them up one at a time, looking at the serial numbers, the seals, the lines in Benjamin Franklin's forehead and ruffled collar. On the fifth bill, something caught my eye. I held it closer, then flipped it over. My eyes widened.

Right above the words ONE HUNDRED DOLLARS and just beneath the depiction of Independence Hall was handwriting. Penned in very small letters of block script was 1700 CHARLES. To the right, underneath the trees in front of Independence Hall, was CINCINNATI, OH.

I reread it twice, then lowered the bill and picked up the ledger, lying upside down to keep it open.

Cincy – Minnie – 250

Who or what was Minnie? And 250 what?

I picked up all the bills and began analyzing them front and back, one at a time. Halfway through, I found more writing in the same place on the back of a hundred:

656 MANSKER N – MINNEAPOLIS, MN

Setting that bill aside, I sorted through the rest and found two more addresses, one in Bayport, New York, and one in Syracuse, New York. I took another drink—emptying the glass—and stood and paced.

Four mobsters, one from Cincinnati, one from Minneapolis, and two from New York had invited me, presumably because they saw my ring, to play poker with them. The second night, they had suggested I bring the cigars—cigars I had found in the locker of a dead man, along with a class ring. Those four mobsters had then lost, over the course of two nights, almost five thousand dollars, asking at the end if it was enough and telling me I'd have better luck than "Jumpin' Jimmy," who had tried to sell to a couple of guys who backed out on a deal. Or was that just a random story? And four of the bills in that five thousand dollars contained addresses, presumably where I would ship the rest of their cigars, them having authenticated me and sampled the product, all while anyone watching—say a couple of overeager FBI agents—would see nothing but some goombahs playing a poker game with a local guy.

Possible?

Very.

Likely?

Maybe.

I went back to the ledger.

Boots – Piggies – 5

I wasn't exactly down with all the cigar lingo, but I'd never heard them referred to as boots or piggies. Stogies, yes. Piggies? Like baby pigs? Or like "this little piggy went to market"? Or . . . as in the Bay of Pigs, in Cuba?

I poured myself another half glass of cognac and looked at the clock. Pushing twelve-thirty. I paced some more, thought through it some more. It made more sense this time. And boots, I realized, *could* be a reference to Italians, from the country shaped like a boot—if Stewart got creative and a little weird with his nomenclature.

Say it was true. Say Angelo Ravello and his cronies had come to South Florida to catch up, swap stories, and "pay" a broker five grand for a down payment and future delivery of illicit Cuban cigars. What were the other entries in Stewart's ledger? It was possible he was brokering more than one deal at once—likely even. But who had killed him, and why? And who did that leave as the buyer for the missile specs if not the mob? Caridad? Stewart himself? Someone else entirely?

Something told me I should know the answer. Something somebody had said, in passing. Maybe two somebodies. Pacing, piano playing, and liquor aside, I didn't have the brainpower to figure it out. I drained my glass, then swept up everything off the coffee table and returned it to my safe. I peeled off my clothes, set my alarm for way too early on a Sunday, and fell into bed only to realize I had left the lights on in the living room.

A pillow over the eyes solved that, and I was asleep in minutes.

THIRTY-ONE

MY ALARM DID NOT WAKE ME UP. MY DOORBELL DID.

I sat up, giving even odds between the feds and Summer. No, more likely Summer given the way they'd left the night before. And even that was hard to believe on a Sunday morning.

I was not decent, so I pulled a white robe monogrammed with an ornate letter G on the breast from my closet and bound it around myself. "Coming," I shouted as the bell sounded again.

The lights were on in the living room. *The* light was just starting to shine outside, which told me it was about six-thirty. I felt my watch still on my wrist from the night before and glanced down to confirm it, then peeked through the peephole.

Diana Berglowe stood on my front porch, wearing a pair of gray slacks and a maroon pullover, terribly casual for her. Her black hair was pinned up in a small bun behind her head, the same frameless sunglasses as she'd worn Friday morning pushed up into her hair, as they had been then. Her face, distorted as it was through the peephole, struck me as pensive.

I tousled my hair and opened the door. "Diana."

"Mr. Shades. I'm so sorry to bother you so early."

"It's no bother," I said, hoping fake charm won out over morning breath. "What can I do for you? Come in, please."

She did, and I offered her a seat, but she declined.

"I tried calling you last night, and . . . you must have been gone."

"I was out," I said, realizing I'd forgotten to check messages. "I'm sorry."

"I've had a change in my departure plans," Diana said, wringing her hands again, "and I was hoping to get the necklace back from you so I can pack before a quick walk on the beach and then my taxi comes."

"Nothing the matter, I hope."

"No, no. Just a change in plans."

"Have a seat, and I'll get it for you," I said. "I'll just be a minute."

"Thank you, Mr. Shades."

I retreated into the bedroom and closed the door partway. While I opened my safe, I wondered if Diana's change in plans was just that or if I should be suspicious. It was too early to tell.

The necklace was still in its pouch, and I carried it back to the living room. Diana had taken a seat after all, at the table. "It's rather warm in here," she remarked as I exited the bedroom. She pushed up one sleeve, then stopped with the other halfway when she saw the pouch. "Oh, thank goodness."

"You were afraid I'd lost it?" I said with a smile.

"No, of course not. It's just . . ."

She stood, and I handed her the pouch.

"Thank you so much, Mr. Shades."

"You're welcome."

"You must think of me as frightfully crazy," she said, putting a hand to her face. "Mr. Shades?"

"Uh, not at all," I said, suddenly trying to process what I was seeing. Halfway between the elbow and wrist, on the inside of Diana's exposed forearm, was a tattoo. While atypical on a woman like Diana, it wasn't unheard of. What threw me to the point that I could barely cover my surprise, was that the tattoo was of a butterfly.

"Well, I really must be going," she said, starting for the door. She stopped halfway there. "Thank you again, Mr. Shades. You've been so helpful."

"My pleasure," I said with a forced smile, trying to steal another glimpse at the tattoo. Before I could, she turned and let herself out.

I stood there for a moment, feeling a little flushed myself, but not because I'd forgotten to open windows before bed. Freddie had confessed that a woman with a butterfly broach had put him up to stealing from the hotel—a woman that, with a little interpretation of his description, could have matched Diana, who, as it turned out, had a butterfly tattoo on her arm.

That could have been a coincidence. Lots of women like butterflies. They're enamored with the things, in fact.

My alarm started blaring.

I silenced it, then stripped off the robe and hopped in the shower. Sometimes I'll spend a while there in the hot steam and spray, thinking. This was not one of those times. I hurried through the necessities, then picked out an old blue and white patterned collared shirt and a pair of khaki shorts. A well-worn pair of Paul Sperrys, used for walks on the beach when I don't want to deal with sand everywhere, and a bucket completed my disguise as a fisherman. I threaded the stem of the most non-descript pair of sunglasses I had, also for discreet situations, between the buttons of the shirt. I grabbed my fishing pole, a simple tacklebox, and my camera, inserting it into the tacklebox. Just in case, I tucked my Colt 1911 under the top tray of the tacklebox too.

I determined I had just enough time to brew a small pot of coffee, and, while it dripped, I reviewed everything I knew yet again.

Was it possible Diana was involved in the deal that was about to go down? Was that why she wanted the pearl necklace, to trade it for missile specs? Was her inability to reach me and get it last night the reason Tony had been stood up at the greenhouse? If so, why would she have ever given it to me to hold onto, or involved me in the first place? Was her fearful, helpless demeanor not an act? Was she a timid spy? Had Stewart's death spooked her to the point that she asked the hotel detective, whom she had originally approached as some sort of cover, to keep the payment safe until it was time to make it?

And then what of Freddie? Why had she, assuming it had been her, paid him to steal taffy and fudge and beer nuts? To distract the resort's manager and Head Security Officer? Same reason she'd talked about suspicious characters and lurking Arabs?

More questions and answers and theories and conjecture, and my coffee was done. A look at the clock on the face of the microwave told me it was five before seven, and time to go.

I poured as much coffee as would fit into a Styrofoam cup. With it in one hand and my "fishing" gear in the other, I set out for the door. I smirked, realizing it was too bad I hadn't pocketed one of the cigars from the night before so I could chew on it like George Peppard's character on *The A-Team* while making my plan come together.

THIRTY-TWO

SUNDAY MORNING HAD DAWNED OVERCAST. BUT WITH

enough slits in the clouds for pinkish-orange sunlight to squeeze through and dapple the water. It also cast the entire sky in a surreal amber glow. With just a hint of breeze, it made for a calm, beautiful morning to be out on the end of the two-hundred-foot pier that extended from the beachhead just north of the resort boundary.

I had stashed the camera, as I'd told Gia I would, in a wood box that housed umbrellas. I had half expected her to be waiting there for me, but the beach had been empty. It still was, one or two joggers down the way notwithstanding. So was the pier, save for one old man at the three-quarter point, two poles in rod holders doing all the work while he munched on an apple. We had grunted hellos, but that was it.

Ten minutes in and I didn't have a bite. Of course, that was because I hadn't used any bait. No good having an act of espionage committed right under my nose because I was busy reeling in a twelve-pound bonefish as part of my cover. I had positioned myself on the right side of the pier, which was shaped like a very narrow T. I was at the serif at the arm of the T, fishing back toward land so I could see what happened. I was trusting my hat, standard sunglasses, and blah clothes—and Tony and the buyer's eagerness to finally complete the deal—to keep me from being recognized.

The only watch I had was a Rolex, which wouldn't fit a fisherman, so I had no way to tell time other than my guess, which was now at eleven minutes in. An old guy, judging by the limp, ambled onto the pier. He wore a yellow raincoat, apparently in case the few sprinkles I'd felt turned into something more, and a bucket cap. He painstakingly made his way to the halfway point on the other side and began setting up shop. I hoped three fishermen wouldn't "queer the deal," as Kevin would put it.

I took a long pull on my coffee, which had grown lukewarm. I looked up and saw a woman in pink pants rolled up above the ankle and a white windbreaker emerge from the hedges that separated the beach from the resort. I smiled to myself, both because Gia was easily identifiable, even from this distance, because of her affinity for pink and her lighthearted gait, and because pink was an awful color for someone to wear when they were going to be hiding.

Her hair in a ponytail, she looked out toward the pier—or maybe the ocean in general, she was very casual—a few times, then up and down the beach once. Then, that quickly, she darted between the dunes and disappeared.

I took another drink and swallowed with a wince. Lukewarm coffee or lukewarm iced tea—I didn't know which was worse. A smattering of sprinkles validated the gimp's choice of apparel. The other fisherman, no spring chicken himself, coughed/belched, and then the claps of the ocean lapping against weathered wood and the caw of gulls took over.

It apparently wasn't my lack of bait. Nobody pulled in a fish as several more minutes passed. Then Tony, presumably, stepped out from the far opening in the hedges. He wore salmon shorts and a light blue knit pullover. He walked purposefully north on the sand, then turned onto the pier. I turned up the collar on my shirt, just in case, a move that was also validated by a few more sprinkles from behind me.

He wasn't carrying anything, and I sneaked a glance at a hundred feet out to make sure it was in fact Tony. I nearly grinned. His hair was blown by the wind, but only partially. A pair of cheap, wouldn't-be-caught-dead-in-them sunglasses were pushed up over his forehead. I concentrated on my fishing pole, deciding it was time to reel it in and check the "bait." I did so, figuring Tony wouldn't be paying close enough attention to see there was nothing but a bobber at the end of my line.

I threw in some indistinguishable mumbling and a few coughs for good measure, then recast my line. In the process, I briefly glanced over my shoulder and saw that Tony had taken up residence in the far corner of the T, his back against the railing. I mumbled again and watched my bobber hit the water. Unable to look back at him, I watched the shoreline. An old man and a dog walked slowly south. A female jogger passed going north.

Then a woman in gray slacks, a maroon pullover, and with her hair in a bun exited the hotel property due north of The Grandeur. Her sleeve was no longer pushed up to the elbow, but I didn't need to see the butterfly tattoo to know that Diana Berglowe had played me but good. She was the buyer; the pearls I had been guarding were the payment. Not a sentimental gift from a former liaison. More likely black-market merchandise stolen by the Soviets.

I wanted to kick myself. Unbeknownst to me, I'd had both the missile specs and the payment in my safe at the same time. But I hadn't then known which parties were involved. Now I had it all before me—the specs, the pearls, Tony, and Diana. And my Colt 1911 in my tacklebox at my feet.

I just had to execute capturing everyone and everything as the transaction took place.

THIRTY-THREE

Diana stopped at the base of the pier and stood

looking at me. Or at Tony, it was hard to tell from a couple hundred feet.

I chanced the quickest of glances over my shoulder. He was staring at her, like this was the climax of *The Good, the Bad and the Ugly*. That made either me or the old fisherman in yellow Clint Eastwood's character. I really should have had the cigar.

My eyes were back on Diana as she lifted a familiar-looking velvet pouch from waist level and held it up. One more flit of my eyes showed Tony removing the sunglasses from atop his head and holding them up. The next thing I knew, she had set the pouch on the end of the wood railing and started walking onto the pier. Out the corner of my eye, I saw Tony go by, walking toward her. I looked back and saw the sunglasses sitting on a small shelf built into the railing of the deck, theoretically for tackleboxes, not U.S. stealth missile schematics.

Like a couple Appalachian duelers—or, more accurately, Cold War spies from opposing countries—Tony and Diana continued walking toward each other, their paces steady. Tony passed the coughing old guy, who was busy muttering at his lines and clueless. Yellow Raincoat was hunched over the railing, equally oblivious.

The wind gusted as they drew within fifty feet of each other. A few spattering raindrops hit me as they met in the middle of the pier, neither casting more than a quick look at the other. Then their backs were to each other, him more than halfway to the payment and her more than halfway to the specs.

I quickly debated my options, and the likelihood that Diana was a KGB sleeper agent who knew a dozen ways to kill a man with her bare hands. I flicked my eyes to the dunes, to see if I could catch a glimpse of a camera lens, wondering if Gia was getting incriminating shots, including with the zoom so that faces and objects would be identifiable.

Diana was two-thirds of the way to me, and Tony two-thirds of the way to the pearls.

I concluded my best bet was to let Diana actually pick up the sunglasses before I made my move. Otherwise, she could claim she had merely come out to watch the waves. I could apprehend her, and still be close enough—theoretically—to threaten Tony with my Colt. Worst case, he got away with payment but the specs stayed out of the hands of the buyer.

As Diana drew nearer, I emulated the other two fishermen and focused on my bobber in the water, at the same time flicking open the lid of my tacklebox with my shoe. Diana was almost to the top of the T when everything happened at once.

Rain—not just sprinkles, but actual rain—started falling with a new gust of wind.

Yellow Raincoat whirled around and started running full speed toward the end of the pier.

A flash of pink caught my eye and I saw Gia emerge from behind the dunes.

THIRTY-FOUR

I FROZE. TORN OVER WHICH SCENE TO FOLLOW.

The wind caught Yellow Raincoat's bucket hat and carried it away, revealing a pinned-up wad of curly black hair. Black wraparound sunglasses were no longer able to disguise Caridad. I should have known.

Her footfalls on the deck caught Diana's attention. A dozen feet from the sunglasses, she spun around to see what was happening, and nearly stumbled when she saw Caridad charging at her like a bull in a slicker.

Tony also turned around. He hesitated, looked back to where the pouch was equally at hand, and then to Gia—camera-less—approaching the pier.

Diana turned back around and hurried to the shelf. She plucked the sunglasses off it and started to tuck them into her pocket. As she did so, Caridad raced past me in a blur of yellow and plowed into Diana. I heard her gasp, then cry out as the two of them hit the railing, the way Denis Potvin might take Wayne Gretzky into the boards at Nassau Coliseum. I wasn't sure if that made me Mike Bossy or Dave Semenko, or the referee whose eyes had to remain on the puck/sunglasses.

Tony shouted, his voice but not his words audible over the wind and gusting rain. He made some sort of gesture toward Gia, then turned and started running our way. Even the old guy—assuming it wasn't Costa or O'Connor in disguise—turned to look at the ruckus.

And it was indeed that. The sunglasses had fallen from Diana's hands, clattered on the decking, and came awfully close to falling into the ocean. Crumpled into the spindles of the railing, Diana used one hand to try to shove Caridad away and another to reach for the sunglasses. At the same time, Caridad tried to wring Diana's neck with one hand and grab the sunglasses with the other. The result looked not unlike a hockey tussle, with a lot of sweater grabbing and flailing and very little actual fighting.

I still hadn't moved, but as their grappling caused them to fall to the left, under the shelf and away from the sunglasses, I took a step forward.

Before I could get to the sunglasses, Diana landed something of a punch that knocked Caridad back. Diana half stood, half lunged for the sunglasses, securing them in her fist. As she stood again, so did Caridad. In a move that had to have taken practice, she whipped off the raincoat, revealing tight-fitting black clothes underneath. Instead of dropping the coat, in one move she spun it around and lashed out at Diana with it.

Diana took a step back, and Caridad charged. This time, like the Great One, Diana was nimble enough to avoid most of the "check," and Caridad slammed into the railing beside her. With a move that clearly indicated tactical training of some kind, Diana grabbed Caridad's arm and twisted it behind her, then threw a punch that sent Caridad reeling. Then, before I could do anything, she scampered up onto the railing and dived overboard into the ocean.

THIRTY-FIVE

CARIDAD WAS NO MORE THAN FIVE FEET FROM ME. TONY

was bearing down on us. Before I could pull myself out of my
shocked daze or he could reach her, Caridad rolled to her feet, shook
out the cobwebs, and looked around. Quickly surmising what had
happened, she too clambered onto the railing and hurled herself into
the waves.

Tony reached the end of the pier and the point of the T. He
looked at me, but recognition didn't flash in his eyes. Instead, he
peered over the edge of the railing, then moved to the far end of the
pier. I craned my neck to see Diana stroking for shore and Caridad
floundering after her.

I stood transfixed as Caridad caught up and swiped at Diana's
ankle. She missed, then caught her again. I turned away as Tony
came back and stood beside me.

Caridad's second attempt to grab Diana resulted in a brief
struggle from which Diana then broke free. Instead of again setting

out for shore, she turned and faced Caridad as she began swimming. Diana threw a punch that turned into a grab and a headlock. The wrestling match continued, this time looking less like hockey and more like a marlin on the hook.

Tony shuffled to the right and around the corner of the T, drawing him closer to the fight. He peeked over the side again. I took a step left as the duo floundered under the pier. They were a mess of flailing arms and churning water, and then suddenly Caridad rose out of the water. Diana surfaced a second later, right into a right hook that snapped her head back. She floated toward a pylon, and I watched helplessly as Caridad grabbed her and slammed her head against the pylon with a crack that echoed over the waves, wind, and rain.

I thought Diana might go under, but Caridad kept her afloat, frisking her—clawing at her, more like. A few seconds later, she pulled back and intently began swimming toward shore.

I was once again frozen. Caridad had the sunglasses with the specs. Diana floated limply in the water. Tony took off running down the pier. I looked to the base of it, not seeing Gia. I swept my eyes up and down the shoreline, looking for pink and seeing nothing. I watched Caridad stroking toward the beach like an Olympian. I watched Diana, half submerged and lifeless.

Save the specs or save a life?

Had I known for sure that Diana was a foreign agent, a Soviet spy or KGB operative, it might have altered my decision. But it was *possible* she was working for the good guys, trying to foil a deal just like I was. Specs or not, I couldn't let her die. So I discarded my hat and sunglasses, kicked off my shoes, and dove in.

She was still limp when I reached her, possibly concussed or possibly dead. I didn't take the time to find out but looped one arm around her and began backstroking toward shore with the other.

Halfway there, she began coughing, choking, and fighting against me. I'd heard of lifeguards kayoing a swimmer in distress so they could actually get them to safety. I managed to avoid that, half swimming and half dragging her back to the wet sand. Then we lay there for a minute, her on her side hacking and spitting water and me on my back panting, as the waves crashed into us.

We got up at the same time, and I was a little afraid she was going to unleash her Muay Thai or Krav Maga on me. But the look on her face and the bleeding gash on her forehead told me she was in no condition to fight. In fact, after just a moment, she wobbled and fell backward onto her rear.

I stood in place yet again, heaving for gasps of air. Caridad, swimming unencumbered, had reached the beach and was long gone. Tony, sprinting down the dock, had reached the beach and was long gone. Maybe they'd gone separate ways or maybe they were fighting in the waves on the other side of the pier. Gia was also gone, as was the pouch from the railing at the base of the pier.

I was oh-for-two. No specs. No pearls.

The rain continued to fall.

THIRTY-SIX

"YOU SURE MADE A HASH OUT OF THIS ONE." SUMMER

said.

I was standing in her office, barefoot, the mucky sand that caked my arms, legs, and shorts having dried. My clothes and hair, for the most part, too. My underwear, not so much.

Caridad had not been found.

Neither had Gia. Her windbreaker, a tank top, and her pink pants had been, at the corner of the property adjacent to The Grandeur. What exactly that meant, I was still pondering.

Diana Berglowe—dollars to donuts that wasn't her real name— was being fought over by the cops and the paramedics, both of whom had arrived a few minutes after we came out of the water. Maybe the old fisherman—the only person who hadn't been playing a part—had shuffled to shore while I'd been saving Diana's life and called them.

Or maybe he was an East German operative under deep cover. Whatever the case, he'd been gone too.

I had made a statement to the cops, by which time Summer had been summoned, along with the manager of the hotel to the north. I hadn't told the cops that Caridad had absconded with military specs, because I didn't really want to spend the rest of the day in a windowless room explaining my actions over the last forty-eight hours. I said instead that I'd gotten wind of a deal going down, been there to observe, and then chaos had broken out. They had bought it. Summer had not and had summoned me to her office for an explanation. Her bull-o-meter was well calibrated, so I'd given her the full rundown.

She shook her head, crinkles of hair flitting back and forth. She looked nice in her lavender sundress, but I tried not to think about it, especially since I was starting to chafe.

"Aren't you going to say anything?"

"You pretty much summed it up," I said.

She took a few steps closer. Not harshly, she asked, "Gregg, what were you thinking?"

"That I could stop the deal from going down, recapture the sunglasses, and maybe catch the seller *and* buyer in the act. And I was right there, about to do so."

"When, what, a catfight broke out and distracted you?"

So much for the non-harshness.

"That's not what happened."

"Really, because it sounds exactly like what happened."

I sighed.

"And it's not just how things played out on the pier," she continued. "You let your feelings for this girl guide you instead of your good judgment. You didn't have to be the hero, didn't have to try to make the perfect sting. You *had* the specs, and the ledger from Stewart's room. Why not tell the police and let them handle it?"

Summer didn't know about my deal with her father and the CIA, as per both of their stipulations. But her point wasn't lost. Substitute "the CIA" for "the police" and she was right. Had I not been trying to provide a happy outcome for Gia—and, truth be told, trying to impress her—I likely would have handled things differently and not made a "hash" of them.

She shook her head again. "I'm disappointed in you, Gregg," she said and turned back to her desk.

I took that as my cue and trudged out of her office, feeling the sting of that rebuke, of her disappointment, more than I wanted to admit.

The sun had come out, so before I went back out to the pier to get my tacklebox and gun, I squinted and set out for my villa to get a new pair of sunglasses. I thought more about what Summer had said as I trekked back. Part of me wanted to argue with her, argue that my plan had been just fine—it was the execution that had failed, largely because Caridad had showed up. But had Gia not been a cute brunette, would I have still opted to try to take down the buyer and seller myself? For that matter, if Gia hadn't looked cute in her pink one-piece and straw hat, would I ever have approached her, ever interrupted the original swap, ever gotten into a poker game with Angie and the boys that set me on the wrong path? Would I ever have met Caridad or thought anything of Diana's pearls?

Caridad.

Presumably she had killed Stewart as a way to get the specs and/or the pearls. But how had she ever known the deal was going down? Unless she *was* the buyer and Diana *was* a "good guy" trying to foil it. That didn't seem to wash though. Caridad's actions didn't fit a buyer, but rather an interloper, a third party. So how had she found out?

The same way she had known of the specifics of the swap on the pier?

I hated being left with guesses and conjecture. I hated even more that I had failed.

For a change, no one was waiting in my villa. I had a quick shower to get the sand and saltwater off my skin, and dressed in a pair of shorts and a green- and white-checked Winchester shirt and sunglasses to match. Then I hiked back to the pier, where my tacklebox was right where I'd left it. So was my fishing pole. And the shoes, hat, and sunglasses I'd discarded before jumping in.

I reeled in my bobber, made sure the gun was still where I'd left it, and packed up. Then I tromped back to the dunes and ferns and fan palms where Gia had hidden. There was no sign of my camera. I checked the umbrella box and found it right where I had left it.

Gia had played me.

I thought back to how things had gone down on the pier, to her emerging from the dunes when she had. She had come toward the pier at the same time as Caridad had turned and started running for the sunglasses. That had drawn Tony's attention, and he'd pointed toward the pouch of pearls and come running. Then the hockey-like catfight had ensued, and neither Gia nor the pouch had been seen again.

I flashed back to the patio of The Coconut Grille at lunchtime, when Frankie had been trying to remember when he had last seen

Gia. Angie had confirmed it was Reno in 1978, then said, "Hello, *mia perla.*"

I didn't know enough Italian to say more than hello or goodbye, but suddenly wondered if *mia perla* didn't translate to "my pearl." Could have been a coincidence, a common nickname like sweetie or honey in English. Or it could have been a nickname for a girl who had a thing for pearls, and who had connived a way to steal a pearl necklace worth hundreds of thousands.

I started walking again, in the sand, but slowly. I remembered Gia meeting me after the poker game and telling me about the time and place of the meeting, which she had overheard from Tony's conversation. I thought of Caridad somehow knowing of it too. I again pictured her taking off running in her yellow raincoat, of the wind blowing off her hat, of Gia emerging from the dunes at just the right time.

Suddenly I pictured the two of them sitting on barstools at some out of the way tiki bar, drinks in their hand, laughing it up. And toasting the sucker they had played to get rich.

THIRTY-SEVEN

I RETURNED EVERYTHING TO MY VILLA, THEN RETRIEVED

the remaining contents of my safe—the locker key, the strongbox with the class ring and the ledger, and the $4,840 I had "won" in poker from the ex-Mafia. I still believed they had been in Florida for no other reason than to buy illicit stogies, but given my track record over the weekend, I wasn't too sure of that.

I pocketed the cash and put everything else in a paper bag. I dropped it off in Summer's office, in case the cops needed it. Presumably, they would be back to resolve Stewart's murder and Diana's assault, and maybe to arrest me for obstruction of justice.

Then, because sitting around and moping would do no good, I took a stroll through the grounds. There were several cute girls sitting by the pools, but I gave them a wide berth. There was also a handsome, slightly narcissistic Italian young man well on his way to plastered at the Circle Bar. I took it his sister had played him too, one part of this equation that didn't bother me. And since I had no proof of anything, I didn't have a way to turn him into the cops so they could sweat a confession out of him and get him to implicate the person who had leaked the specs to him in the first place. "Hash of this one" didn't begin to describe it.

Sweet Creams wasn't open yet, so I turned right, past the firepit and over toward the shuffleboard courts. I had a hunch I might find four old guys sliding discs around, and sure enough Angie and Frankie were battling Nicky and Vinny in a match.

"Hullo, Shades," Angie called. I got similar greetings and waves from the other guys, indicating they had no idea what had gone down at the pier with Angie's grandchildren. That made it more or less unanimous.

When he saw my face, Angie's smile waned, and he leaned on his cue. "Something wrong?"

I reached into my pocket and pulled out a roll of cash—$4,440 worth. "I came to bring this back."

The four of them crowded in with nervous looks around.

"I think there's been a mistake," I said. From my other pocket, I took out the four Benjamins with printing on the backsides. "I don't have anything to send to you all."

Angie frowned, the same stern look on the photo Costa and O'Connor had showed me Friday morning. Nicky looked anxiously left and right.

"Maybe I'm completely off here, but I think you guys lost this on purpose as payment for some more cigars."

Angie's eyes answered in the affirmative even though he said nothing.

I explained briefly how Martin Stewart had been murdered, how I had found the cigars and ring, how I had thought at the time—as had the feds—that the four men were up to something nefarious and thus had gone along with playing in the game to catch them. They pressed in closer, and I wondered what would happen in a fight between four old, angry mobsters with shuffleboard cues and a strapping young man with a wad of their cash.

"I put the pieces together last night, and I don't have any more cigars or access to them. And I have no interest in turning you guys in over cigars, but it wouldn't be right to keep your money."

Angie stared a hole through me, then turned to the others. Frankie grunted, and Vinny nodded slightly. Nicky invoked a saint.

I swallowed.

Then Angie's face broke into a grin. "Keep it, Shades. We'll win it back on our next visit."

I looked to each of them. "You're serious?"

"We are."

"And maybe," Nicky said, his voice a little raspier, "when the time comes, you can do us a certain favor."

He waited only a beat—but long enough for me to break out into a sweat—before cackling with laughter. The others joined in, and Angie slapped me on the back. "He had you going."

I exhaled and then smiled along with them.

"Come on, get in this game," Frankie said. "You can take Vinny's place, see if you can make this a fair match."

"My place? Old man," he said, shaking his cue in Frankie's direction, "we're fixing to make a comeback."

"Ha!"

I held up a hand. "I'd love to, next time," I said. "But I'll leave you to it. You're sure about the cash?"

"Positive," Angie said.

I nodded. Bail money, maybe.

Before I turned to leave, I asked with just a sliver of hope, "Any of you happen to see Gia this morning?"

Three of them shook their heads. Angie said, "Not since dinner last night." He winked. "Figured she'd be spending what time she had left with you."

Nope, I said to myself as I turned away. *When you're done with a tool, you have no need for it anymore.*

THIRTY-EIGHT

HUNGER CAUSED ME TO SWING BY THE COCONUT GRILLE

to get a chicken cordon bleu sandwich and some fries. The solitude of my villa was calling me, so I took my lunch to go.

I camped out on the deck, slouched in my chair, feet up on the railing, and my Styrofoam take-out container on my stomach. While absentmindedly munching—and crumbing on my shirt—I thought through every move Gia had made.

I was convinced it had been my idea to come up to her—there's no way she could have known her hat would draw my attention. But had *she* been the one to initiate the sunglasses swap? Had she played me that well? To what end—to throw off the exchange? To buy time? To manipulate everything?

Had she been trying to figure out who the buyer was, assuming she had known—however she knew anything—that Tony was to be paid in pearls, or had she known it was Diana? Had she and Caridad been working together, or had she found a way to use Caridad? Had *she* somehow killed Stewart?

I replayed our conversations, particularly as they pertained to his death, to what we had found in the strongbox at the Amtrak station, to *our* plan to catch Tony and the buyer, to *my* belief that it was Angie and the gang. How much had she manipulated and put thoughts in my head?

With disgust, I reached for my longneck of Coors.

I heard a crunch in the grass and turned to see Summer come around the corner of the villa.

I raised an eyebrow, took a swig, and looked away.

"You didn't answer your door."

"I didn't hear it."

She climbed onto the deck. "You don't drink beer."

"I do on occasions."

"What's the occasion?"

I slowly panned my head her way. "You want something?"

She held up a small, bulky manila folder. "Courier dropped this off for you."

"A courier?"

Summer nodded.

I took the envelope by the flap. "And *you're* delivering it personally?"

She bit her lip and turned toward the railing, loosely clasping her fingers behind her back. "I realized I might have been a little rough on you earlier. I wanted to apologize."

"You have nothing to be sorry for, Summer. You were right."

"Still, I'm sorry I wasn't . . . more delicate."

I actually smiled. "You were fine, but apology accepted."

She took a breath. "If you want some company, Collins is out of town all day. I'd be happy to hustle you at pool."

For all our bickering and contempt, we'd long ago settled onto something of a truce over the billiard table. In part because it helped us both relax or cope with stress and in part because neither of us could find anyone else to give us a decent game, we'd made the lounge on the ground floor of The Grandeur something of a DMZ and played more than a few friendly games of eight-ball.

"Thanks," I said, "but not today. I'm going to lay low."

"Okay. Don't beat yourself up, Gregg."

"Thanks."

Summer nodded, then turned and walked away. I waited until she was back around the corner before setting my takeout container on the stand beside me, next to the bottle of Coors. I sat up, dropped my feet, and tore open the end of the manila envelope. I reached in and pulled out a pair of cheap, ugly sunglasses, black with pink stems. I sat up even straighter. Then stood and went inside.

I set the sunglasses on the table and looked in the envelope. There was a single sheet of folded paper, and I dropped the envelope and opened it.

Shades,

I'm sorry I played you. I knew before we ever came to Florida that Tony was selling something, albeit not what it was. I have a weakness for pearls, and when I eavesdropped and learned that he was to be paid with a pearl necklace, I looked for a chance to make my move. Then when you showed up and said you were the hotel detective—and had those super cool sunglasses—I saw my chance.

But it's like I told you, the Ravello family, with one obvious exception, are patriots. Once I learned what was at stake, I couldn't stand the idea of my idiot brother getting away with treason. So after he switched the sunglasses last night, I switched them again. The pair he was wearing were fakes, and the pair those two dipsticks fought over on the pier were fakes. I'm sure they've figured it out by now. I trust you'll do the right thing with these, and if it means Tony getting in trouble, well, he should. I hope they'll also keep you out of trouble.

I also hope you don't hate me. If it matters, if I had just been a girl on vacation with her brother and grandpa and you had complimented my hat, the weekend would have played out the same way it had—until this morning.

I left a note for Grandpa Angie too. I'm not going back to Long Island, at least not now. I've been saving for a while, and now is the perfect time for me to see the world. I don't know where it'll take me—maybe someday back to a cozy resort in south Florida and a cute guy with excellent fashion sense. If not, I won't forget you, and I hope you won't—and don't want to—forget me.

XOXO,

Gia

P.S. You would have *loved* my carbonara but you'd never have tasted it, because I *would* have beaten you at tennis . . .

I read it twice.

And then, because I'd developed trust issues with females over the last two days, I retrieved my blacklight and verified that these were indeed the sunglasses with the missile schematics on the lenses.

Then I sat down at my kitchen table, the sunglasses in the fingers of one hand and the folded letter in the other. I tapped the edge of it on the table, again and again, thinking.

I tend to be a little pragmatic. And I realized several things.

Once I turned in the sunglasses to the CIA and they did their thing, I would be—mostly—out of trouble.

The U.S. would still be in possession of its missile technology.

Tony Ravello would quite possibly get what was coming to him, even if he hadn't been caught red-handed.

Angelo Ravello and the boys were out five grand but had enjoyed the best smokes of their lives, and maybe learned to play the cards a little more than their bluffing skills.

"Caridad" was in the wind, but had nothing to show for her efforts but a pair of cheap sunglasses no self-respecting woman would be caught dead in.

Diana Berglowe had a head full of cobwebs and likely a scar, but nothing to take back to her superiors—whoever they were.

The Soviets or the East Germans or the Bulgarians hadn't gained any intel.

Gia had the pearls, and while she was at least a minor league grifter and thief, I'd rather them be in her possession than the aforementioned parties'.

And I had a fun weekend and memories of Gia in her hat and tennis dress and hunter green gown to look back on. And maybe a lesson or two learned.

I finally stopped tapping the edge of the paper on the table. I folded it again and tucked it in my shirt pocket. I put the sunglasses in my safe until I could arrange to deliver them to my bosses, then stuck the letter in the top drawer of my dresser.

Then I went back out onto the deck to finish my sandwich, this time with a smile on my face. It had turned into a beautiful day. I lived in paradise. And the next weekend, the next wave of guests, and the next adventure were just around the corner.

AUTHOR'S NOTE

MY INSPIRATION COMES FROM UNUSUAL PLACES. THE

idea for *Shades* dawned on me while watching a rerun of *Banacek*, starring George Peppard as a nattily attired insurance investigator who solved capers while wooing clients and suspects alike. In an instant, I thought about creating a series around a hotel detective who, among other things, is a sharp dresser and a ladies' man. Like with so many ideas, it became a snowball rolling downhill, and somewhere became an homage of sorts to my favorite 1980s TV shows.

Setting a novel in a previous century is a challenge. I was two at the time *Shades* takes place, so my recollection of the time is lacking. I relied on those aforementioned TV shows, the always trustworthy internet, and the fact that half my readers are in the same boat as me. But there's a benefit too. A 1980s detective actually has to detect—he can't Google his way to a solution. He has to run to a phone booth (a what, you ask?) instead of whip out his iPhone, and he has to know how to read a map, not just listen to it. (He also has to be attracted to women with *really* big hair and belts in weird places, but hey.) And Cold War villains (read: Soviets) still make the best fictional antagonists.

There's risk in writing a "period piece," especially in a culture of Snapchat and TikTok. (Are those still things?) But classics seem to be in too—Hollywood can't make an original, it's all reboots. So I figured, why not?

If, like me, you'd rather watch Tom Selleck than Jay Hernandez, Scott Bakula than Raymond Lee, or Richard Dean Anderson than Lucas Till, I hope *Shades* (and future installations) resonates with you. And if you associate the Eighties with glam bands, the *Challenger* or Chernobyl disasters, and VHS, I hope the throwback vibes won't be too strong. Lastly, for those of you who know the era of Reaganomics better than I do, forgive the inaccuracies. I hope they don't distract from the story.

-Nate